Canadian social philosopher G. V. Loewen is the author of over twenty books in diverse areas such as ethics, religion, art, education and politics. He was a professor for a quarter of a century in Canada and the USA. This is his first short story collection.

Dedicated to all those in the real world who recognize themselves in the heroes of the pages that follow: Godspeed.

G. V. Loewen

SHOOTING AT MORALS

FULL METAL FICTION

AUSTIN MACAULEY PUBLISHERS™

LONDON • CAMBRIDGE • NEW YORK • SHARJAH

A CIP catalogue record for this title is available from the British Library.

ISBN 978-1-78823-363-7 (Paperback)
ISBN 978-1-78823-364-4 (Hardback)
ISBN 978-1-78823-365-1 (E-Book)
www.austinmacauley.com

First Published (2017)
Austin Macauley Publishers Ltd.
25 Canada Square
Canary Wharf
London
E14 5LQ

Acknowledgments

To Chris Crutcher for exposing the ongoing suffering of children. To Guy Vanderhaege for literary inspiration, and to my wife, Jennifer Heller, for everything else besides.

Contents

Whether we immoralists do virtue any *harm?* – As little as anarchists do princes. Only since they have been shot at do they again sit firmly on their thrones. Moral: one must shoot at morals.

Nietzsche (1988:26 [1889]).

1. First Person Posthumous

After attaining my medical degree, I immediately found myself behind my regiment which, given that the second Afghan War had already broken out, proceeded ahead of me into the Khyber Pass region. By the time I had caught up, they had been involved in the now notorious Battle of Maiwand, and indeed it so happened that I was fatally wounded at that very battle, my orderly having failed to get me back to our own lines.

But seriously, folks. I actually was killed in an intersection in downtown Toronto, riding my bike. I had the right of way, of that I am sure. Someone careened through the red. Probably drunk. At any rate, I wasn't given the leisure to stick around and find out. I know the exact spot, but I am not reproducing it here lest the reader think that I wrote this narrative ahead of time as a kind of bizarre and whimsical suicide note. In any case, I could not have planned my death in this way unless someone could prove that I knew the driver of the vehicle which struck me and killed me instantly. Could he have had a secret grudge against me, you might wonder? Perhaps I *did* know him, a figure from my past, who recognized me while we were both flying along in different directions in a city I have but frequented an odd few times. No. Alas, it happened just as it did, and though I am here to reflect, not so much on that final moment, but what it means to have experienced it both before and after, as both prehumous and posthumous, I very much wish that I were not.

Let's get that part down straight right away. I don't want to be dead. I wasn't that old. Indeed, I fully expected to have at least another twenty odd years left with which to do as I pleased. The whole book circuit thing I took up against my better judgement. Vanity, I suppose, now that I look back on what got me into this permanent fix. Launching now here, now there, flying between cities, always on the go, pushing my wife to join me no matter what her own work dictated. Squeezing exercise in at less than ideal times and places. I wouldn't do it again, had I the chance to rewrite history. But that's the whole point, I guess. I can't, and neither can you.

And I guess you're all wondering what it's *really* like. You know, on the 'other side', as it were. Well, don't get too excited about it. I'll get there when I'm ready. For now, let's suffice to say that it has been singularly uninformative. Durkheim was apparently right when he asked, *Why should death confer special privileges or powers?* Unless you think my continuing ability to write is something more special posthumously than prehumously. Maybe it was never particularly special even in life. The only question for me at the moment is how long this is going to go on for. If one really does have 'eternity', whatever that may mean, at one's disposal, then I guess the world is going to eventually be inundated with my writings. 'Haven't we suffered enough?' you might cry, but you might just be crying in vain, after all. Not that I'm simply going to just continue to write and write, and not try to do anything else. 'Special powers' or no, at the very least, we know 'eternity' to be an indefinite period of time. That probably means that one could put a great deal of practice into things and thus get some other abilities than what one already possessed. Practice is everything, by the way. Sometimes I've been accused of being a 'genius', but really folks, all genius is, is simply this: ninety percent organization, nine percent egotism, and one percent, 'I've just read twenty books, oh, wait a minute, I have an idea.' That's all there is to it. I'm thinking that some of you like the idea of romantic and transcendental genius simply because it actually does take a modicum of effort to write book after book, even if no one reads them. You can't just dither around and accomplish much of anything in life. So I think we can dispense with inspirational genius along those lines.

By the way, another thing that has not yet happened in the much vaunted 'afterlife': I haven't met any of my historical heroes, speaking of genius. Nope. Not a one. No Mahler, no Nietzsche, no Beethoven, no Goethe, no Whitman *et al*. And I wasn't really expecting to, as a matter of fact. Why would figures such as those be hanging around waiting for *me* to show up and glad-hand them? If what has apparently happened to me also happened to them some years ago, they're probably way ahead of me, off exploring other planes of existence, perhaps, or maybe they waited around for each other and are playing poker somewhere. A game with elite cultural stakes, no doubt. Either way, I won't be joining them anytime soon. That said, I haven't met any of the villains, either. I haven't met anyone, in fact. Himmler hasn't sidled up to me and informed me that it was a person of Jewish descent who ran me over – on purpose no less – because *they* were worried that I might eventually break into their little intellectual cabal. You know, like Zizek did. Rest easy, folks, I wouldn't have believed him if he did. I *would* ask him why he's still at liberty even posthumously. A born schemer, he might reply that I was actually in a place that I didn't think I was going to end up, and just didn't know it yet, because my crimes against humanity were relatively benign. Nevertheless, he's there to keep me company every so often, along with all the rest of them. That might rattle me a little bit, I have to admit, but I would try not to believe him on that score either.

Pending future observation, I'll let that line of thought rest for now. I *will* let you in on something odd I have noticed so far, though: all the bodily functions and feelings that one has while alive are either gone or have been transmuted by some existential alchemy. Case in point. It's been about ten hours, so far, judging by the sun in the sky, and I haven't needed to use the washroom, to eat, to sleep, although it's the middle of the night. I'm not cold, or hot, don't need my reading glasses – and with one exception, I can't hear anything at all – *and* no sexual feelings of any kind. Well, you might say, you're dead, after all! Not exactly the sexiest position to be in, unless you're into necrophilia. You'd need to be that and have a Ouija board, because no one would want my misshapen body parts after they were torn apart by that lunatic in the intersection. I can understand, a little, desiring the corpse of a youthful maiden – isn't that the gothic stereotype? But trust me, I wasn't that even in the prime of life. So no takers there. But what I *meant* was the usual desires of one's own sexuality. Here I've still got the entire internet

16

at my fingertips, for instance, and I have experienced no compulsion at all to check out the latest in any erotic genre. That's probably a first. Yes, this is the time for true confessions, isn't it, if there ever is such a time. Maybe some secrets should go to the grave, and that one did. But here I am again! Did you miss me?

So whatever form I am in, it's singularly vanilla. Doesn't want to eat, drink or fuck. Either with itself or with anything else. Now I would give my life – easy to say, you snicker, now that he doesn't have one to give – to be back with my loving and lovely wife. I have winced my way through these not so final hours worrying about how she is taking all of this. She's at least quite a bit richer for it, by some, well, perhaps I shouldn't say just how much, that's not really fair, is it? It's really none of your collective business, anyway, so you can all stuff it on that point. But otherwise, it's going to be tough. Not that I was God's gift to women in life, quite the opposite. Maybe some of that will come out, whether or not people still believe in not speaking ill of the dead or some other such nonsense. And indeed, they wouldn't be speaking ill if they told it straight. It would just be what it is – empirically verifiable observations about me as friend, lover, confidante, and serial pest. There's a lengthy string of women strung out behind my wife who, if they haven't forgotten about me entirely – and doesn't everyone hope for the best case with regard to prior romances? – then in all likelihood sneer and snort in my direction. Oh, well! You can't please all of the people all of the time. What they can't deny, is no matter how they feel about me now, or even right after they got rid of me, or I them, is that for whatever period of time, day after day and night after

17

night, I owned their tails and could do just about whatever I wanted with them. Notches on my belt, so to speak.

Well, from now on things are going to be different. If I can't even get interested in the internet I'm certainly won't be chasing the girl-angels themselves, should any happen along my way. But there's something else going on too, that I should, in the interest of science as is said, perhaps pass along to you. You know those prickly chills you get from time to time, maybe in reaction to the contrived *frisson* of a B-movie or, more profoundly perhaps, in those alpha states, transitions between sleeping and waking when you think someone, or something, is close beside you, either ready to communicate the muse or do you a mischief? Well, since I've been dead my form, my 'body', if you will, has had that feeling very strongly, and seems to *be* nothing other than that feeling, in fact. I don't know what it means, of course, and I hope that none of you are expecting the philosopher to come up with all of the big answers to all the 'big questions' that are oft touted as the be all and end all of thinking. That too is nonsense, by the way. 'What is our duty?' Goethe writes, 'The demands of the day'. Absolutely correct. Our fragile mortality dictates this to every one of us, and those of you who find they need to ponder the abstracted ululations of previous epochs as if they had some reality to them need to get a grip. I am further convinced of this given the state I am in at the moment. It doesn't do one any good to question the terms 'state', 'in' and 'am' in such situations. It is what it is, whatever it may be. It doesn't have any meaning at all, except the one we might give to it. So far, I am content to hedge my bets. Indeed, if you want my advice as a dead guy, you should do the same *before* you come my way. Start today.

Yeah, I know. The cosmos is profound in and of itself. I agree, to a point. It's always possible to imagine an Indra's net of myriad universes, each a gem in its own right, but not truly profound unless seen as a whole. Only a God-like vision could apprehend such a panorama. Oh yeah, haven't seen any sign of *Him* around here, either. Not that someone like me would be high on his call list. Hell no. Aside from all the women I've stuffed over the years, there's all the people I didn't help when I could have. Right down to that little old lady in Hamilton a few nights ago, struggling home with her cart full of groceries in the ice and cold. We could have stopped our limo and stuck her and all her stuff in the back seat comfortably, drove her home and patted ourselves on the back. That said, my wife didn't think about it either, let alone the limo driver, who's not paid to think about such things in any case. So you get my drift. Some more advice: given that there appears to be some form of regret or remorse in the afterlife, I'd try to cut your list down as much as you can while you still can. Sounds like another bloody Christmas Carol, but why not? Don't do it because you fear eternal or divine judgement. Utter nonsense that. Don't do it even for others. Do it because you *can*. Make it an otiose extension of the will to power or something, if you need even that kind of metaphysics to hang your hat on. Metaphysics is a crutch, anyways. Yes, we all have something of the sort. And just because I preferred the original human structure of consciousness, the so-called 'transformational' metaphysics to the later incarnations, didn't mean that I was aloof to human concerns. Quite the contrary, in spite of what some critics may now say about myself and my work now that I'm gone, I was no different than any of you. Well, except for *some* of you atheists out there, who think that because you claim to believe in nothing that you don't have any beliefs at all. Just a note to self; haven't met any such atheists around here yet either.

But I digress. The funny chill down your spine kind of feeling. Yeah, it is a little odd. I always wondered about it when I was alive. I was one of those people who, being a romantic – hey, just ask all those women! – could supposedly sense things that others couldn't. But then the question was, what things? Why? How? But in fact *most* people have odd experiences in life. Once again, we attach whatever meaning we feel makes sense to us. Most of it is the tripe we soak up from the consumer version of culture. Angels and demons, spirits and aliens. Unbelievably unimaginative. Even though it seems to be the case, at least for me, that the reality of this 'other' dimension is even more dull. Maybe *that's* the answer you've all been waiting for. Whatever you think during life about the afterlife is what happens to you when you die. You can make it all up, and the most exciting eternity will befall the most exciting person. The coolest to the coolest, the most vanilla to people like, well, you know who you are. That makes things a little more socially real. We can now ask such questions as 'well then, who *is* the coolest person on earth?' I have read that it is the professional golfer, Miguel Angel Jimenez. You know, the guy who brings two bottles of red and a few cigars to the practice tees before a tournament. The guy who collects Ferraris and Lamborghinis. The guy who has very smoky girlfriends even though he's well into his fifties. Yeah, I could live with *his* afterlife, if our premise turns out to be correct. Cool really does mean cool too. I mean, like, as in cucumber cool. That's why that other great collector of Ferraris, the virtuoso guitarist Yngwie Malmsteen isn't quite as cool. He's too excitable and frenetic, it appears. But his afterlife would still be cool, don't get me wrong. I've got a great photo of him doing his thing in front of a blazing row of Marshall stacks on my desktop at this very moment. Supposed to inspire me to not only do my best, but also to damn the torpedoes, which has got to be his motto. Jimenez's motto would be, 'what *is* a torpedo?' as he sails on. That explains the difference between the two pop culture denizens, and that's what I mean by being truly cool.

I'm very much not cool. Not that I'm totally uncool, but I'm probably getting close. Hey, wouldn't only a big-time dork be able to sit down and write his own epitaph *after* he were dead? I mean, who gets to do that? I guess some of you will think what I'm doing here is cool, and it has its moments, but really, I am writing this for your benefit, not for mine. I just thought you'd be grateful, or at least interested – I'm not expecting anything in return for this effort, by the way, it's just like all the rest of my writing; read it or leave it, it's all the same to me – for some description of 'the great beyond'. Of course, it might well be better to have some corresponding insight, but it looks like you're just going to have wait and see if you can glean some for yourselves when your time comes. It will, by the way. And sometimes when you least expect it. I was going to say that I'm living proof, but that doesn't quite fit the bill. We don't really have an expression, at least in English that communicates precisely what I am at present. Let's just say that I'm proof of the foregoing, and leave it at that.

It being established that I am not cool, but not a complete geek, I should move on to a few other notes. Aside from that tingling feeling, I have, since my demise, been able to hear a low rumbling drone, like a more diffuse version of the chants of those famous Buddhist monks, you know OOOOOOMMM! etc. This has not let up. I have no idea where it's coming from or what it 'means', to use that word again. I have wondered that it might be the sound of the cosmos itself, now that I am somehow a different part thereof than I used to be, but this is sheer speculation, and I don't really even have any right to share it with you. But I know my audience. You're expecting something from me. I can't just prattle on about nothing even though that's pretty much what this place is. Don't be disappointed, folks, maybe you're afterlives will be more like Jimenez's, or at least Malmsteen's.

So, tingling all over, like the tingles themselves have replaced my body, and the sound of the cosmic monastery continues. Oops, there I go again! Forget I said that. What else? Well, aside from the desireless non-being with which I regaled you earlier, the only way I can tell time has passed for the still living is by observation of your world. I don't feel the passage of time, I guess is what I'm trying to say. Okay, now that *is* something worth mentioning. All the more reason why you, readers and critics alike, might be in for a lot more of me over the coming years, your years, that is. Hah! Now *that*, for a writer and thinker really is a little slice of paradise. Forget the cuter than cute young girl-angels. In a dimension with no time, how much work could one potentially get done? Everyone who said I was washed up a few years ago take warning, you're about to be flooded! A veritable diluvian diversity is coming up, to add to this recent and unpublished set of stories I wrote over the last couple of weeks. No Ouija board needed, it appears. I just hope my wife keeps this machine, or something else I can use, and isn't too spooked about it. It's okay, honey, it's just me. You're rid of me if you want. Don't hang around just because I'm, after a fashion, still here. Just set up a machine somewhere in your swanky new house – I mean it, sweetie, go to town, you've waited a long time to have what will truly be your own life, and I've often felt a little bad conscience about it; yes, this *is* the time for true confessions after all (the more public, the more credit) – and forget about me. You recall me saying, my dear, how I used to say I couldn't wait to die! I didn't mean it as it sounded, I think you knew that. But what I *was* trying to get across was the absolute gratitude I felt toward you day in and day out: so much younger and more beautiful than myself, how could I have deserved someone like you for so long in my life, that sort of thing. It's not just pretty words and you're not just a pretty girl. So now go to town. You can do and be whoever you want to be. In fact, that brings me to my final point today, folks.

Being what you want to be seems to be the order of the moment over here, wherever this is and whatever I am. But you know, it's not so different than back there. Yes, I know there are material and symbolic limits. Who am I, a privileged SOB by birth and gender and ethnicity and even to a certain extent, class and education, to call out those who can't exercise the free will of human nature. And even this might be a mirage. But, as I always used to tell my students, 'I don't know if free will exists, but if you believe that it does, you will change the world.' Another thing – and excuse the homiletic quality of this stuff, the afterlife kind of gets to you in that tired way, I suppose – *Make your lives worth dying for*. That's another duty of the day that I'm pretty sure Goethe and Co. would have approved of. I used to tell my students this all the time too, and now I'm telling you. Heck, maybe if these luminaries ever show up, I can ask them what they think about it all, but I'm not holding my breath, if you get my meaning. But as far as the rest of it goes, well, nothing to report probably means nothing at all. I know David Hume killed the 'old god of morals' back in 1739, even though it took almost 150 years before someone recognized the implications of deicide – and another century or so before they named a band after it! – but like a lot of things in life, you've got to maintain your alertness. Just like government, unions, universities, schools, families, just because things are going well for the moment doesn't mean you can turn your back for an instant. Power really can corrupt, but it doesn't *necessarily* do so. But what is always part of that corrupting power is the perversion of morality. And that means to take morals as if they were really carved in stone. Well, folks, they're not. That's just how it is, and you'll have to deal with it in whatever way you think best.

History is the ultimate argument against morality.

But now I note with some astonishment that, floating up above me in a corner of the room there has appeared a young woman, gesturing for me to follow her. She is quite adorable and she is also quite naked. And you can't really refuse an invitation like that, now…* [can you?].

****

24

*Editors' note: The ms. breaks off here, and we have inserted the final two most likely words at this juncture. The story was left as an open document on the author's computer which itself had been left on. The author's wife suggests this was rather out of character and indeed, the story has been written with remarkable prescience given the facts of the case as known. It was also clever in a number of logistical ways; for example, the date of the document was also found to be after the event of his death. But the remainder of the stories to which the author has referred above have yet to be discovered.

2. Cry Sheep

"A fake ID? Why the hell would I need one of those?" Max was sitting in Greenblatt's surgery. The specialist was peering into his eyes.

"There's a lot of new, young talent coming into town these days. People who want not only to keep their heads, but to use them as well." Max's doctor was referring to Arab speakers fleeing Islamic State. Intellectuals and artists, writers and critics. All of the kind of people that would not last a second under any reactionary regime.

"Aren't they all sponsored anyway?" Max queried.

"Not all of them." Greenblatt was now peering into his ears. "I don't know why Eschig sent you over here, Maxy, there's nothing wrong with you that a good screw wouldn't solve." Max groaned. "You remember Schlotzky? Well, he got himself a gig at the consulate downtown. Always brown-nosing Wasps, not worried about being stung. It finally paid off."

Max was unimpressed. How much did diplomats make, anyways?

"So, given that their *gelt* sucks, he runs a little side-business, a little moonlighting service, if you get me."

"Providing new ID, etc."

"Yeah, etc., etc." What did any of this have to do with him? Max thought. Okay, so maybe he could hire some of this new blood and pass the Arab off as the Jew. They all had the same skin colour, mostly.

"I'll look into it. Izzie never liked me, though."

Greenblatt was now peering up his nose. "No, but what is done is done. You stole the girl and married her, and look what that got you?" The doctor paused, then: "Speaking of which, nose hairs aren't so sexy anymore, Maxy, you know what to do." Max winced, thinking about the tears he would shed prying and tugging. "What you need is to loosen up." Greenblatt was now peering at his waist. "Elvis the Pelvis you are not. My idea: Vegas. A week, maybe ten days."

"They'd ruin the place in that time." Max was referring to his magazine business, no, empire, no, perhaps grand duchy, that was it. Too big to keep track of on a daily basis, too small to make sure New York didn't get another *goyim* mayor.

"And so what? How many guys like you are out there?" Greenblatt had a point. Max's existence wasn't particularly profound, and God knows, his magazines weren't.

"I'll look into it." Peering was Greenblatt's specialty, not his. But, recalling this conversation on the red-eye to Las Vegas, Max Heller felt that he had, ironically, been once again a follower in order to cut loose; 'Loosen up', as the good doctor had suggested. Well, now that

Constance had walked out on him, this was as good a time as any. His parents had warned him about marrying an Aryan girl. But Izzie had been so goddamned arrogant about the whole thing it had become a source of enduring pride to him, even when it went south a couple of years ago because Max had been shagging some of the new talent at work. Actually, their best talent was quite literally on the cutting room floor, but it was good to find that out early on, before too much investment had been made and well before their prissy names had become a fixture in his publications. God!

The pilot announced the final approach, a little huzzah went up from the passenger cabin, as usual, and they presently touched down. Stepping into the heat, it wasn't the sights of Vegas that first impressed, but the sheer weight of the absurdity of plunking over a million people down in the middle of a desert. Goats, all of them, Max thought, including me for being here, for wanting to be here of all places. Then the sights, sounds, and the masses of people began to kick in. Paroxysm, catharsis, cathexis, Vegas was all of those rolled into a frenzied heap. But no one took anything seriously out here except having fun. And all the fun had here stayed here, so the unofficial city slogan went, as if Vegas was intent on jealously guarding not its secrets *per se*, but its reputation as a black hole of supposed indecency and incivility, a refuge from all morality and an insulation against transcendental suasion. Sodom and Gomorrah had nothing on Vegas, especially since Yahweh had seen fit to ignore it, though Max, an unbeliever at birth, simply thought this evidence of God's sense of humor; play dumb all the while partaking in it. God knows God himself might be in this bustle somewhere, finally stooping to earth when Babylon resurrected itself somewhat east of Eden. He might have been on his very flight, for God considered himself to be a cultured being, and the only spot of culture in the Western Hemisphere was New York City.

Sitting in the hotel casino cafeteria, Max was brooding on the forty-three messages he had received from his staff in the last two hours. Most were utter nonsense, and he ignored them, but a few were important enough to require a curt reply, and one or two were personal enough to require some reflection. In the midst of this, he found himself no longer alone. A decent looking woman of about forty was sitting across from him at the small table, drinking gin and peering at him. Not again. Max raised his eyebrows and opened his mouth but she stepped in first:

"Looks like we're finally alone," she offered. Max raised his eyebrows a little more, and closed his mouth. "Vegas is much more fun with company than without it. If you don't like what you see I have plenty of others." Max was a little unmanned, but not for long.

"Look, Miss, no offense, but I've only been in town thirty minutes. I need to breathe a little, know what I mean. Eat something and get half-looped." Max was doing his level best to try to impersonate a tourist but it wasn't working.

"You sure look like you're trying to relax, Max," she said, without knowing his name. Max blinked and forced himself to put his phone down, still face up. The woman looked hard at him, almost glaring. Max flipped his phone face down and looked up.

"Satisfied?"

"You're sure a *schlep* if you think you can satisfy a girl by putting your phone down for a minute. Why, I didn't even feel it vibrate, got nothing at all." Max looked hard at her, now.

"Are you Jewish?" he asked, a little surprised at the epithet.

"Are you kidding?" then, realizing she might have offended, "I mean, no, I wouldn't try to pass as..." Max broke in, finally gaining some higher ground.

"Yeah, I am. But who cares, it's not like I'm orthodox, sitting in a casino chatting up a strange *goy* girl from who knows where."

The woman brightened up a little and said, "My name's Janine. I'm a Madam. I still like some myself on the side if the guy is right. Someone like you, you're what, maybe close to sixty, but still solid. Not much hair though, but since Patrick Stewart that doesn't matter." Max thought it more appropriate to reference Telly Savalas here, of all places, but said nothing. She continued, "So, which is it? Me or one of my girls. Or two or three?" Max winced, thinking that, though he hadn't had sex for a couple of months, one Vegas hooker would be plenty to handle.

"Listen, uh, Janine," a pause, then Max broke out a little: "For God's sake, you don't waste any time out here, do you?"

Janine looked a little sheepish, then said, "Like I said, Vegas is much more fun with a friend or two."

Especially when I'm buying, Max thought rather pettishly. But after all, what the hell had he come here for in the first place?

"Someone like you, married for a long time, I reckon, bored, maybe in business, but getting too old for the girls at work to be over-interested in. Maybe they have you because they are thinking promotion, maybe they don't have you because you're not the boss. Whatever. You're here. Once you stepped off that plane the world changed. Maybe you haven't quite noticed it yet?"

Max didn't think the world had changed. Not a bit. Prostitution was legal here. So what? It was basically legal in New York too. Fuck me, he thought, my wife became a salaried prostitute about ten years ago, when romance, itself lasting a good long time after all, flickered out. That was what she had been to him, though she would see it as indentured servitude.

"So, I've got a big line-up tonight. It's a week-night so you can take your pick."

Janine wasn't going to give up, Max realized, so he finally sighed and assented, "You know, I like you. A persistent business-person. But I'm a little shy. I think I would feel somewhat, you know, rusty with someone like you. Maybe you could send me someone younger, or just plain young." Someone who won't make a fool out of me, Max added to himself. Indeed, he was beginning to feel a mighty fool in any case, negotiating something that seemed shady in a place where the brightest of lights shone on every act. Janine nodded.

"What's your room number?"

Max blinked again. He hadn't realized that this was it, he supposed, that soon he'd have to put his money where his mouth barely was, and then his mouth where his money was, so to speak.

"I'm near the top, penthouse B." What the fuck, he thought. Impress them a little. Maybe he'd get stiffed but the thought of relatively fresh meat on his doorstep gave him a sense of empowerment and also entitlement. Maybe this was what sex for sale was all about. Not the sex, because one could generally pick that up anywhere, but the idea of service. Service with a smile.

Janine nodded and said, "I thought so. You look wealthy." Then, once again, a look of consternation. "I didn't mean because I knew you were Jewish, and all, you know, I…"

Once again, Max had to break in.

"Forget about it," he clipped rapidly, putting on his best Brooklynese just to tease her. "Don't be a *schlumpf*, a *schlemiel*. Like I said, I'm a Jew from New York. Himey-Town. The best thing about it are the delis, the bagels, the pickles, for God's sake. So next time you see me, think pickles."

Max couldn't stand people who apologized for a history they had no part in. The Christians invented guilt, he supposed, so that they could practice atrocities and then atone, to themselves, afterward. But most people weren't even Christian any more.

A youthful middle-aged woman in Vegas managing a run-and-gun brothel. Very upstanding. Nor immune to the call herself. She'd probably been a hooker and then cut out on her own. Gutsy move. Her eyes looked a little washed out, now that Max had had a chance to look at her more closely, but she wasn't an addict. No, they had a glint about them that was not purely pecuniary. There was something more to this woman than met the eye, his eyes, at least. If the eyes were the window to the soul, as Aristotle had supposedly said, then this woman still had one. What it was made of was at present beyond his ken. Maybe he should have become a psychiatrist like his father wanted him to. Following his footsteps, he might well have arrived at this moment ten years earlier. Well, what was done was done. Janine had abruptly risen.

"I'll meet you upstairs in ten," was her parting utterance. Max was left as he had started, except the world, inconspicuously at first, had begun to change.

****

A rapid knocking at the door summoned Max from his phone. Opening the door, he beheld not only Janine, but a much smaller woman, no, a girl. Max raised his eyebrows in what had become a signature manner in the years running a media business – how many young writers had wilted in the face of his eyebrows, he found himself wondering for a moment, the pair of them a silent but deadly duet – and then the two guests were inside. The door locked. The younger one said nothing. Didn't even gaze around the luxurious space. Janine seemed a little nervous.

"So, it's three grand for the whole night, one gee for two hours," she stated shortly.

What the hell, live a little, Max thought.

"So I'll take the deal, then." Max had known his best successes by taking the deal. His talent was recognizing it before others did. Here, there was no risk of other's competing, at least not for the 'whole night'.

"Cash only," was Janine's only response, dropping a sports bag on the floor. So Max had figured. So Max had visited the bank machine. His daily limit was well above the requisite funds involved. He had bought champagne just to be nice. He had ordered some room service and stuck it in the fridge. Caviar and sushi, but also breakfast stuff, just in case the night dragged into the morning. Max realized a little late that he was mimicking what he and Constance had always done together. Sex and more sex, early on, and then eating chocolate mousse cake in bed, naked, then so revitalized, getting down and dirty once again. Such memories were already getting in the way of the present reality and Max let them do so. But after Janine had left him with this waif, his and his alone for the next ten hours or so, Max began to feel a little depressed. At best, the girl standing awkwardly in front of him, shuffling her feet and swaying a little, as if there was some kind of fresh breeze in the room and the penthouse floor had become the deck of a sailboat, could have been his wife five years before they met. God, maybe ten years, Max now thought, as he began to actually pay attention to what Janine had chosen for him. Who, not what, Max chastised himself. Hookers were people too, you know. Then, without word or warning, she was naked and on the bed.

"Hey!" Max expostulated, astonished and embarrassed at once.

The girl blinked up at him, completely without shame, and said acerbically, "What's the problem, mister? You ordered a fuck. That's why I'm here. You don't want to

34

fuck me? I can call Miss Hendricks back and get you a refund. Get you one of my friends, if you like that better." She was nothing if not sarcastic. It oozed out of her little lips, much like Max imagined her fluids oozing out from her corresponding pair. That is, if she was even aroused, which Max seriously doubted. In the pause that followed this first barrage, the girl had reloaded and fired again. "Don't tell me you need to go take your meds, old man. Come on, I've had nothing all day. You *can* get it up, can't you? Jeez, if you can't get it up for little old me, then you can't get it up for anyone." She was now preening, turning her tiny rear end towards him and looking back, grinning slyly. She winked at him, and sighed heavily, reaching back and fingering the very lips that Max had analogized about just a moment before. And like a judgement, Max was aroused. How could that be? He asked himself. This girl looked like she was still in school. Then, "What school, Max?" He was talking silently to himself but the voice in his head was suddenly Greenblatt's. "This girl is a hooker. She doesn't go to school." He imagined for a moment the juvenile fantasy of the high school confidential. "She's going to school you, though," Greenblatt finished up. Max had to say something.

"Uh, I'm not sure I want to have sex immediately." How lame. The girl's disgust at him was written all over her face, indeed, all over her entire rake, from the lanky but strangely beautiful legs of a not quite left-over adolescence to the narrow hips and barely 'a' breasts, to her perky chin and cupid's bow. Her tousled but ratty hair framed a face that spoke not only of usury but something else that Max couldn't place.

Then, as abrupt as had been her nudity, she said, "Oh, Gawd, all right then!" She had grabbed a couple of pillows, placed them square on the bed and leaned herself over them so that her waist was resting on their mound and her slim and almost boy-like posterior was shining up at him. This provoked yet more arousal on Max's part, but also something untoward and unexpected.

"What the hell?" he said under his breath now that he could see her more clearly. The girl didn't move. Her posterior was stained with bruises, some healing and brownish and some a little more recent and multicolored. It was now Max's turn to be disgusted. "Does Madam beat you if you don't perform?"

"Of course not, idiot," was her only response. What the fuck had happened then? Max found himself groping around, out of his depth. Actually, he now realized that he had been out of his depth since Janine had accosted him in the cafeteria. "Well, come on. The stuff is in that bag." Max didn't move, but looked with astonishment at the girl, then the bag, then the girl again. She was rapidly getting agitated with him. "Look, if you don't want to fuck me, then you want to discipline me. It's either one or the other or both. Nothing else ever happens, so get busy. Like I said, the stuff is in the bag. Its part of my kit, comes with the price, know what I mean." Then, as if she had sensed something in her memory, she blinked back a tear, and said much more softly, "Please mister, use what's in there only, would you?" She was now meek and gentle, indeed, Max thought her to be more scared than nervous. He was totally and utterly at a loss. But he had to do something.

He decided to take the plunge. But when he reached over to pet her head she flinched a little. This froze Max and he heard Greenblatt's unintelligible warning in his inner ear. Max then decided to find out what was going on here. No matter that time was wasting, as it were. He didn't come to Vegas to abuse women, well, not really. Not so directly. Not as a requirement of the rite of passage he had belatedly given himself to accomplish. He strode over to the sports bag and opened it up. Reaching in, he again froze. He couldn't believe what he thought he was feeling. He peered into the bag and saw that it was true. Yes, there was the odd dildo in there, the odd *schlong*, but mostly the objects were leather and plastic. Belts, straps, and rods. A ball gag. Some ties and old pairs of pantyhose. A veritable potpourri of S and M articles, but nothing too serious. This must have been what the girl meant by her imploring him to stick to the 'kit'. Some guys must bring their own 'stuff'. Like booze, a young girl might not be injured by beer, but give her vodka and watch her fall. Someone else, not too long ago, had plastered her with something other than what was available in the official sports bag, 'sports' rapidly becoming defined more and more loosely. That explained the bruising.

Max was starting to feel queasy. He looked up at her. But she again spoke first: "I'm obviously a bad girl. More than a brat. So go to town, mister. You're my step-dad and I've broken my curfew once too often. Or, you're a teacher in, I don't know, Texas or some other godforsaken place where they hate kids. Come on, you know I deserve it." She bounced her little bottom up and down on the pillows several times. She was the very picture of cuteness but Max was not convinced. He sat down heavily on the bed beside her. She continued apace, however. "Or you can simply put me over your knee and do it the old-fashioned way. A lot of guys like that, at least to start with. Warms things up, you know, breaks the ice, gets the blood flowing." Max stared down at her, looking so woebegone that she had to stop and change tacks. "Oh, big deal, come on baby, I like it anyway, I want it. I need it. It makes me horny. I'm your little sex-dolly, after all. This is just foreplay. That's all it's ever been." She was trying to assuage what she imagined was his guilt, the kind of guilt at least some adults might feel after they had assaulted children, their own or perhaps others. Her voice was soothing but she was still sermonizing. Max was almost at the brink of leaving her on the bed, backside turned up, naked and alone. But it was this thought, the aloneness, that stopped him. *This* is what he had seen in the girl's manner earlier. And, by god, this is what he had seen in Janine's eyes as well! So now the question was, why?

"I'm not going to spank you much less whip you. It's absurd. That's not sex, it's violence. I know nothing about you and I'm no judge of your morality and behavior. After all, I'm the one sitting on the bed with you, aren't I?" He was beginning to speak as if he was speaking to his own daughter, more or less estranged for some years.

"Sex and violence go hand in hand. What is penetration but a violence. You have to push yourself into places to get anywhere in this world. A hard slap gets people's attention. I had some guy in here from Canada a week ago. He told me spanking kids was illegal there. Wonderful. I was born here." The real reason she was laying on her stomach was that she probably couldn't sit comfortably, Max thought, looking again at the kaleidoscope on her backside. Clearly it wasn't Johnny Canuck who had done this to her, or was it? Maybe because they couldn't do it up there some of them came down here to get their licks in.

"Who did it to you, uh, Miss…"

"I'm Starr. Just call me Starr, with two 'r's." Max was already too far gone for even that.

"What's your real name, sweetie?" he gently prodded. The girl sighed and shifted onto her side, rolling off the pillows.

"Alyssa," she said softly.

"And where are you from, Alyssa?"

"I'm from Arkansas. You won't know the town." Max was pretty sure she was right. He had never visited the old south, and not just because he had a Jewish background.

"What the heck are you doing here? And, for that matter, how old are you, anyway?" Max, the more he had seen of her, the more he compared her nudity with the overdone makeup on her face, the more on edge his nerves had gotten. The whole thing about her being a stand-in for other people's students, step-daughters, nieces and what-have-you had just made things worse. He had to ask.

"I ran away from home at twelve. My father was no different from my clients. Well, except for you, of course, weirdo."

"So how long have you been working here?"

"Maybe two years." She looked him straight in the eyes. Oh my god! Max suddenly felt the full gravity of the situation. It was as he thought. But how could it be?

"Can you do something for me quickly, sweetie? Can you go into the bathroom and wash all that stuff off your face?" Max was hoping against hope that the girl's memory wasn't too accurate. Or maybe she meant she had only arrived in Vegas two years ago after sojourning in other places. Or maybe she meant that she hadn't been a hooker for some years before becoming one, or…

"Here, is this better?" The girl had re-entered the room, her faced looking cleansed and more or less fresh. The dark circles around her eyes had lightened considerably in their natural state. She half-smiled at him, looking a little sheepish. She was no longer the professional. But it wasn't better. It was infinitely worse. Because Max had now realized that Alyssa was exactly the age she had implied.

"So you're fourteen," he said, barely audibly. The girl frowned at him then pouted.

"So what? Sixteen is legal in Nevada. I can look and sound older than that. I've got tits and a pussy, I've got an ass that guys love to beat the shit out of. I've got a lot more energy than your wife does, and fuck her and fuck you and fuck the world as well…" Alyssa had suddenly lost it and was crouched in a ball on the penthouse floor balling her eyes out. Holy Christ on a crotch! Max was beside himself. He was instantly down on the floor with her, clutching her to him and holding on tight. The girl didn't resist. But it was like no hug he had ever given anyone in his life. It was like holding a sack of wet Kleenex. There was no - how to put it? – there was no human response. The girl was an object, shivering and mewling in his arms. But she didn't reach out for him, didn't clasp him to her. She just knelt there, abandoned even in his embrace. He let her kneel there, seemingly for half-an-hour. Her sobs gradually died down. He lifted her up off the floor and set her back down on the soft bedding and, ever so reluctantly, let go of her. Then something happened that Max was not expecting. The girl reached back out with her hand, seeking his.

"Thanks," she said simply. Another lengthy silence. "Don't feel too bad, huh, mister, half the time I get off on my job. It can be fun, you know, if the john isn't a bastard. I mean, I know what he's here for, and I know what I'm here for, so there's really nothing more to say about it."

"Except that it's illegal big-time and it's also immoral." Could Max play the hero? No, he couldn't.

"Don't be a prudish motherfucker. A girl is a girl. Sex is sex. How many people can say they like their job even half the time? Do you? What are you, anyway? Big money, big heart, sure. But what are you really?" The girl, that is, Alyssa, Max reminded himself to refer to her with her actual name from now on, was starting to get serious.

"I run a media company. I'm from New York. I'm married, well, separated. I have a daughter who is close to thirty and who I never see. I'm lonely and wondering what the hell I'm doing with my life. That's why I'm here. Not for sex *per se*. and certainly not to abuse a child." Alyssa looked up at him with slightly more interest, even concern.

"Welcome to the club," she uttered. "What do they call guys like you? Mid-life crisis thing, is that it? Yeah, most of you come here to do all the shit they wanted to do to their daughters but couldn't get away with. Maybe their wives were watching, maybe they had a guilty conscience. Either way, that's why me and my friends are here. An outlet for a pure society that ain't so pure." Max was taken aback at Alyssa's perspicacity.

"Uh, yes, well, I never hit my daughter or my wife, for that matter." A little smirk from Alyssa. "I never even thought about it." ("Are you sure about that?" – Greenblatt again.) "Well, I did think about it, dammit, but I never did it. I'm a normal guy, uh, Alyssa, not a criminal. I'm moral. I follow the rules. I just wanted a chance to loosen up a little."

"Well, here's your chance," she said smiling mischievously again, and without makeup, looking not even fourteen. God help him, Max thought. There was no way this was going to happen.

"I said loosen up *a little*. You're a lot," he stated with finality.

"Aw, shucks, mister, uh…"

"Just call me Max. That's my real name, I promise."

"Okay. So, I better call Miss Hendricks and find a replacement. Otherwise you're going to go home empty handed, or, maybe not empty handed but with your hands full of the wrong stuff." She thought out loud, brash and outrageous. Max even smiled a little.

"No. I'll call her myself. I need to have a little talk with her." Alyssa giggled.

"Huh, that's what a lot of guys say to me before they start whipping my bare butt. Come to think of it, that's what my dad always said to me before he started in. Funny how those 'little talks' always ended up with yelling and screaming, not talking." She was now speaking more to herself than him. Max didn't want her to see his eyes, now welling up with tears that were never, ever shed either at home or at the office. This lonely little waif, if even real in a city of the surreal and even the unreal, was tearing into him like no one else had ever done. He knew he needed to do something radical. He had come here to loosen up, and by god he was going to.

"Got any siblings?" he asked her, dragging her out of her impending moroseness.

"Alison, my little sister followed me out here. But Miss Hendricks said she was too young for the trade and got her into foster care. I don't know where she is now but it's probably in state." Max was dumbfounded. Janine, full-time madam and part-time social worker? Now more than ever he needed to speak with her, and immediately.

"Well, we need to find her then," he replied. Alyssa gave him a strange look, but dropped it. After Alyssa had texted her boss, with no details, it was about ten minutes before she arrived. She came in with some trepidation.

"Is there a problem?" she queried evenly.

"We need to have a talk, downstairs, in the bar."

"A 'little talk'." Inserted Alyssa with a little grin.

Janine rolled her eyes, then motioned Max out the door. She turned at the last moment and stated sternly to the girl, "Stay put."

Alyssa groaned, snatched the remote from the console and flung herself back down on the bed, without a thought to dressing. Max found himself in the elevator. Janine was not meeting his gaze, so he left it alone for now. Presently, sitting in a secluded spot in the hotel bar, no kids in sight, he opened up with, "So what exactly are you? Hero or villain?" And then, without waiting for her response, but reacting to her opened mouth, he continued: "And no, don't tell me I ordered 'young' so I got young. You know damn well that's not what I meant." Or did she? Max wondered, given her usual clientele. Janine sighed but said nothing. Max thought it best to get this over as quickly as possible. "So, how much?"

"For what? To change girls, no extra charge. Same fees and times apply."

Max grimaced. So it was villain.

"No. I mean to take her. To take her for good." It was Janine's turn to do the eyebrow gymnastics.

"I thought you weren't satisfied with her. Guess I was wrong. You sure you know what you want? Starr is a real petulant little brat. Not always going to be in the mood for your needs, I expect, if she's no longer being paid up front." Janine elaborated, but Max's grim face stopped her cold.

"No. I'm taking her with me. Call it an adoption. I'll pay you. Call it a severance package. I know you've got me black and I've got you. It's a stalemate unless you take this offer. I'm willing to go to the wall on this but I bet you're not." Janine looked as though her heart had stopped. Then, without warning, she leant across the table and kissed him on the cheek. She lingered, and when she withdrew, her own cheek was stained with a few tears. She blinked, and then tried to get back to business.

"I need fifty." Max's eyebrows raised again.

"I assume I can write you a check this time?"

"Of course. A girl's got to make a living, you know." Then, "Oh shit, I did it again, didn't I?" Max, who had been thrown over by Janine's unexpected reaction and then recovery, almost smiled.

"What exactly are you, anyway?" he persevered. Janine's response left him wondering what world he had been living in:

"I started as a social worker. But you know what that's like. Social Services is more concerned with reproducing their own employment situation and easing case worker's loads than with kids. They think that the more kids they dump the better, and aren't that concerned about quality. I jumped ship about ten years ago to work on the other side of the tracks. To get in the trenches. In spite of my training, nothing I knew had prepared me for what I saw." Janine paused to wipe her eyes again. "I rescue the minors and the hardest luck cases when I can. I have a reputation here now, after over a decade. The pimps and madams who don't want trouble direct the children to me. And there are a lot of them. More than you'd think. More than I thought too. Then, I try to gauge the business and 'place' the girls if I think the people can be trusted. It doesn't happen anywhere near often enough. The money I take from these placements allows me the freedom to rescue other girls. Their original contacts often want a fee as well, though mostly it's not that much, because they're handling hot potatoes. One trick with a minor even out here could get them busted for ten years. Not good for business, so to speak."

"So how do you get away with it?" Max wondered why he had looked like a good mark.

"Call it intuition, experience, whatever. I know the signs having worked in the service. I can smell a pedophile from a mile away. They're almost all parents anyways. You might be surprised, but the guys we get here don't have that interest really, they just never got it on with anyone in junior high and they think that their masculinity is still threatened by that. One shot and their done. They might even brag to their friends that they fucked a sweet sixteen out in Vegas because that's the legal age of consent. What they don't tell their friends is that they paid for it, because *that's* not legal, even here." Max nodded slowly. This *was* news. "Then they're done and you never see them again. If I do, I know something's up. The red flags hoisted out upon their return, or if they want a series of dates, or if they want to try it on again with multiple girls etc. But it doesn't happen that often."

"So the girls are actually relatively safe with you?"

"Safer than almost anywhere else, especially in their own homes."

"But it's good return, even so."

"Yeah, it is. But I give the girls a full half. They have their own bank accounts in their own names off the strip, in a place that does that kind of business. Run by, well…"

Max couldn't help but chuckle, and finished for her, "Run by a misunderstood old Jewish guy who wants to show his God that he's not that bad."

"Woman, actually," Janine replied, with a slight look of mischief in her eyes. "But the rest of it, you're probably right." Max sighed. What a place! No wonder what happens in Vegas stays there. It has to. It has nowhere else to go.

Janine continued, "Let's get back upstairs. After you pay me, I'll get her set up to go with. Good thing it's a domestic flight. I have faked being 'Mom' to about forty girls so far. I've had to drive to every town in the state to get them photo ID."

Max suddenly recalled what Greenblatt had said to him. He suppressed a smirk. That bit of information was about to take a different turn than what the good doctor had imagined. He couldn't wait to see Greenblatt's face when he brought his new daughter in for likely her first medical in years, maybe ever. Then he winced. And what would his friend and confidante find then? Fatal STD's? Maybe this whole thing was crazy, after all. But he felt he had committed. Besides, it was clearly the right thing to do, even if Janine imagined Alyssa was going to have to serve him just a little over the years. Then Max had to mentally withdraw a sneer, not at Janine, but at himself. If she'd even been seventeen, Max asked himself on the elevator ride back up to the penthouse, would he have refused to take her? He couldn't honestly say no to that proposition. Next question: what was the difference between fourteen and seventeen, then? State variance in official non-contractual age of consent wasn't it. Max finally had to give in and say that the relevant threshold probably had something to do with a man's first conquest. Or his first serious rejection, as Janine had suggested. Unless you were a real criminal, and most men weren't in the same way most people weren't, after all was said and done, then that must be it.

Opening the door, they walked in and found Alyssa had vanished.

****

Alarm bells were going off in Max's head, but they must have been nothing compared to what his accomplice was feeling. Looking at her, he saw that Janine was on the point of panic. She yelled loudly, calling the girl's real name over and over. They were on the point of running back out when the closed door of the spa opened wide and Alyssa, naked as always, but this time covered with soapy bubble bath, stood there glaring at them.

"What the fuck do you want?" she said.

Janine was too relieved to speak. Max didn't think it appropriate to enter into this part of the process so he said nothing, trying now not to sexually admire the same waif that had moved him to such compassion just about thirty minutes ago. So the three of them remained in an awkward tableau for a few moments more, Alyssa's glare getting more severe, and Janine's relief gradually relieving itself from her visage.

Finally, the girl declared, "I'm busy. I'm locking the door. I'll be out in thirty," mimicking her mistress's declension of the passage of time. She was just about to shut the door when Janine jumped into action and stuck her foot in it. Alyssa gave a little yelp and stood back, as her Miss Hendricks pushed her way through. Then Max heard her stern voice: "Who the hell are you? Get out, now!" A pause. "I said, right now, buddy." Now Max acted. He entered the steamy surroundings of the en-suite spa, and noted, through the fog, a handsome young fellow sitting in the quadruple Jacuzzi tub, looking arrogantly their way. He didn't move an inch. Then, Alyssa sidled past them both and slid languorously back into the waters from which she had emerged. Inevitably, she turned and stuck her tongue out at them. Janine was tougher than all of that, though, she strode right up to the side of the tub and glowered at its undinal denizens:

"You…" she said, pointing at the young man, "Are not a customer."

Then the bathing poster boy for Nascar finally spoke, "Money's on the table under the tablecloth. Two grand was what the girl said. Two grand it is, in cash. We'll be done in the time allotted, that is, if you leave and close the door behind you." Janine had already dropped her sword-like simmer from the now paying, if still unofficial, customer, and had turned it on the girl. She met her gaze, but said nothing. Janine kept at her, the silent knives of stereotomy cutting Alyssa up and serving herself back to herself on the plate of her own making. Then, she turned on her heels and began to stalk back to where Max had been left, washed up on a foreign shore, awaiting a rescue of his own. But astonishingly, Alyssa wasn't quite done.

"I was bored, for fuck's sake. He's hung like a fucking horse and I'm going to ride him 'til I'm faint!" At this Janine turned around and looked like she was going to pounce on her cheeky charge. Alyssa again, "But I'm going to milk him dry beforehand, so don't worry about it." She said less obtusely, as if trying to cajole her mistress into thinking only what a good little business person she was. Once again, Janine retreated, this time for good.

Outside the spa Janine sighed and looked a little ashen-faced at Max. "See what I mean?" Max suggested that she would no longer have the opportunity for such spontaneous adventures but Janine shook her head. "Max, you're going to have to let that go sometimes. These girls are what they are. They've been made and I don't think they can be entirely remade. After a few years, of course, it won't matter as much. But all you can do has probably already occurred to you. Health, education. Passport and driver's license. Food, clothing and shelter and maybe a shoulder to cry on once in a while. Otherwise…" Max nodded slowly once again and looked down. When he looked up again he started and let out a low whistle, for in that short time Janine had slipped out of nigh on near everything she had been wearing and was advancing upon him. This time, Max let it happen. As she tore off his clothes, she said, "I just wanted to thank you for doing what you're doing. Besides, you can't come to Vegas and leave without having sex with someone, it just isn't right. It's not how we do things down here."

"It's not good for business," Max echoed.

"It's not good, period," Janine stated affectionately. Max was surprised at how good it had felt, after about half an hour. Indeed, Janine was not even reminding him of Constance. She was clearly her own woman, and Max, to his surprise, was in turn just beginning to become his own man. He turned to her as they lolled in the dreamy after-scape of a vivid unreality, and suggested that they raid the larder, open the champagne, etc. "Wait for Alyssa. She can join us. After being with Studs Terkel in there, she'll be ready for a bite of something more nutritious."

Speak of the devil, no, not quite. It was 'Studs' who appeared first, wearing only boxer-briefs, but still looking every inch the man he had intended to be. Why had someone like this suffered from missed opportunities in his youth, Max wondered as he sauntered past their bed and grabbed his other clothes. A late bloomer, he supposed, or maybe actually an introvert that turned into the life of the party when naked with a teenage girl. Most guys might well do so, Max assented to himself.

'Studs' then turned, and queried of them matter-of-factly, "Any more like her?"

Janine smiled sweetly.

"No. But as she's our daughter and just fourteen, we can deal direct." At this, the fellow blanched several times whiter than his usual colour and fairly flung himself out the door. They could hear him running down the corridor to the elevator, in the same state of undress as he had presented himself to them. Max and Janine couldn't help but burst out laughing. Even Alyssa's sudden reappearance didn't abate their newly jocular mood.

"No surprise here. Two oldsters attempted sex and realized what a big joke it was," she sarcastically opined. "But in the room just beside them, two thoroughbreds went at each other until they could take no more." She then sighed melodramatically, falling back against the door and stretching her entire length up its frame, clasping her hands above her head and looking up as if beholding a vision. She continued to assail them. "Finally, a real man. My bottom red only from the heat of the shared waters of love, my eyes in tears from the steamy delight of his throbbing…"

Janine finally cut her off with some reproof, "Enough, little girl. Max here is taking you home with him. As you can't fly naked in this country, I suggest you put something on and join us in a little celebration." Alyssa's eyes widened and she stared across the room at Max. Then, leaving behind her professional persona, ran over to the bed and threw herself on him, knocking him back with the force of her leap. She pawed at him and grabbed his remaining hair.

"New York, New York!" she cried out. "So you had second thoughts after fucking the old girl, did you? Well, I can tell you, you made the best decision of your life, Mr. Maxi." At this, Janine gave her a swift swat on her no doubt still tender backside and she winced. She rolled away from them and feigned the victim, "What the fuck, mother hen?"

"Mr. Heller here is serious. This isn't an extended vacation. He's adopting you. We've already arranged it. You won't see me again after tomorrow. Go and get yourself a life, missy. A real life." Alyssa looked like she was about to fall over.

At some length, she thought out loud, "Good thing I just got nailed the way I did, then. Phew." Then she slowly returned and reached out for Max. Her eyes were now fully opened, allowing him to see for the first time the extent of the damage extant in her youthful soul, but as well, the fact that the girl had still, in spite of this, a soul not only present but still pregnant with the future.

****

Alyssa's soulful eyes were filled with wonder as they traversed the downtown of Max's home, after deplaning and finding a cab. The trip itself, taking place a couple of days after their first meeting, had been filled with plans to find her sister and bring her to New York as well. Janine said she could help, but that she could not herself be party to the transaction, as that would endanger her ability to act as a free agent in other such cases. Child Services could not know who she actually was, or rather, who she had been, if she was going to continue to work in the 'trenches'. All told it took a couple of months, but as soon as Alyssa had settled in, she had been able to actually talk to her little sister, Alison, on the phone. It turned out Ali was in Reno. The twelve year old had been moved seven times in two years, and had considered herself lucky enough at that. It was a lot easier to get her relocated than it had been for her big sister. Max winced a little as Alyssa, who couldn't help but discuss her recent experiences with salacious relish, went over their first doctor's visit for the umpteenth time:

"And did you see the mother's face when you told him where you picked me up?"

Max nodded, It *had* been a little amusing, even he had to admit, recalling it while sipping port in the den with his new, almost adorable if utterly irrepressible, daughter, who insisted that she be allowed to drink along with him on every private occasion. The unflappable Greenblatt had almost fallen over when Max presented the little ruffian in his surgery, and then looked like he was going have a cardiac arrest when he found out about her origins.

"Maxi, baby. Look, I've got a thick schedule today, can we do this some other time?" Max had shaken his head. "For God's sake, Heller…" but then Greenblatt had relented. He did the exam after Max had left the room. Alyssa had teased the poor specialist throughout, with questions like, "So what's your youngest patient, Doc? Have you ever fucked a virgin? When did you first have sex, anyway? How come you didn't pick gynaecology?" and the like, so that when Max was summoned back into the exam room, with Alyssa still quite naked on the table, having flatly refused to wear the examination gown, Greenblatt pleaded with him to 'take her away'.

"Take her down to Schlotzky and avenge yourself on him. Leave me in peace."

Max told Alyssa to get dressed and wait in the lobby. The fact she actually had waited for him was something she also returned to when Max had, over the ensuing weeks, gotten a little frustrated at her attitude. But at that moment, his only concern had been for her well-being: "Yes, she does have a few minor infections, but nothing fatal. Two years a hooker, Max, reminds me of what I saw in Thailand. For that matter, India too. Fuck me, Africa as well. Christ, Max, the whole world wants to work this way. No wonder God is dead. He didn't die of pity, like superman said, he must have killed himself." Max mused on that one for a while, heading home in the car. Alyssa chattered non-stop about the sights and sounds. She had turned into an overnight connoisseur of fine food and even wine. That latter was Max's fault, and he winced again. Apropos, Alyssa's slurping up the last of her port brought him back to the present. Without apprising himself about what she had been babbling on about, he simply broke in:

"So Alison is coming next week. How do you feel about that?" Alyssa's face suddenly stopped its motion, and the colour for a moment drained out of it. She was clearly recalling some other, less pleasant and less amusing memory.

"When she showed up at the pimp's place in Vegas. It was before I had left for Janine's place, you know? It was a couple of days before she came and took us away with her. I was so scared. I thought the guy was going to hire her, know what I mean. I thought she was going to be working out the way I thought I would, but at ten years old. Like Thailand. It scared the shit out of me. But I hadn't told him that she was my younger sister. When he saw her, he nearly hit the roof. It was he, after all, who was more scared even than us! Then it was kind of funny, for a while. Then Janine showed up and took us away, I didn't even have a chance to say goodbye to her, Hendricks got her out of town so fast." Now Alyssa was tearing up. Max went over to her and this time she pushed into his embrace and held him tightly, gently sobbing into his chest. Thank god, thought Max. Real feelings. We're not dead yet. God gave up on us too soon, maybe, he figured, going back to his previous line of thought.

"I hope she still loves me, after all we've been through. At least she didn't have to work out like I did. At least if she was beaten, maybe it was just once or twice." Alyssa was now breathing heavily and all the blinking in the world didn't stem the little stream of tears that had flash-flooded her deserted cheeks and flowed around her stifled lips. Max held her close, petting her head. No flinching this time. She was his in an altogether different and wonderful way. And a healthy one, too. Max was determined not to make the same mistakes with these two youngsters as he had done with his own. Dora hadn't even phoned him in over a year. He was vague on the details, but Max had learned that in general, he simply hadn't put enough time into her. He was always at the office. Dora was more or less a piece of furniture, for his wife had her own career as an intellectual. Shit on them, he thought. But at least Dora was her own person, well-ensconced. She might not have had her father but at least she had her father's networks. His half-baked idea of parenthood was now going to come out of the oven full-bodied and full-blooded, and it started right here, each day.

When Alison arrived at the airport, two young female flight attendants fawning over her, Alyssa shrieked out her name and ran like lightning over to her dear sister. Alison at first didn't know where the sound had come from, but as Alyssa bore down on her she dropped her bags and a large stuffed lion she had been clutching and ran forward as well. They met in a joyous collision that had one of the attendants in tears – no doubt Alison must have told them at least part of their story – and left Max beaming. It was the first time in his life that he knew, for certain, that he had done the right thing. And to think what kind of situation this joy had come out of. To think what he was planning to do and how self-absorbed he'd been. And to think that overcoming the ennui of his normal life could be accomplished by breaking a few taboos that weren't even taboo in the place he had gone to break them was more than a joke. Not only was the joke on him, it was on everyone who, while living as part of the world without living within its essential envelope, who lived with people and not because of them, and who imagined that life was something one worked through without recourse to the entire history of the human endeavor, had in fact stopped living, as he had done. Now, with not one but two bundles of youthful energy and vivaciousness coming towards him, their mutual smiles at once turned to one another in exuberant excitement, then turned upon him in compassionate triumph, Max knew that his lease on life had been renewed.

A few weeks later, dropping the girls off at their well-polished school, Alyssa, after waiting for her sister to get out ahead of her and take a few steps toward the campus, reached back into the car and grabbed Max, kissing him on the ear and whispering, "I love you." Then, after a pause, and with a mischievous grin, she added, "Uh, '*Dad*'." She then winked and stuck her tongue out at him, and ran after her sister. Oh, Christ, Max laughed to himself, remembering what Janine had said about remaking such a girl. Well, maybe it wasn't so bad after all. Maybe what really mattered is that he had learned that what passed for morality was not only what people were willing to put up with, but also a benchmark reminding people that they couldn't always do everything they wanted to all the time and remain fully human. Why he had done what he did, Max had only been certain because of what he had seen in another. It hadn't come from the inside out. And, as he drove off, mentally marking the time at which he needed to return to pick the girls up again, he finally understood that it was only what was *outside* that really mattered after all.

3. Second Date

The first date had gone swimmingly, just swimmingly. Emily repeated this to herself several times as she held on tight to the time and place arranged for their second meeting. It almost seemed that the whole world had changed overnight. There was much evidence for this claim, she decided, beginning a list. First of all, the hem of her dress. It was a good four inches higher than anything she had ever worn. Above her knees, for goodness sake! Though just. And the colour of her tights. An alluring velvet burgundy. And the fact that she was wearing nothing underneath them for the first time in her life. Well, except for dance class, but one had a leotard over top so that didn't count. She could feel their luxury against her skin, her calves, thighs, posterior, mons, and even, blushes, her lips. But she wanted to feel it. It was soothing and exciting at the same time. Those were the same two feelings that he had given her, simply sitting opposite her at lunch. His voice was soothing, his words exciting. And here she was, sashaying her way towards another encounter. How the world had changed!

After all, it had been ten years since that incident at prom. Surely that was enough time to recover. It wasn't pleasure either that was the issue, she thought. How many pillows had she humped in the interim? Actually, it was more the number of times rather than the number of pillows. She had had her favourites, the current one being a fairly stiff velvet body pillow. She blushed a little as she recalled that very morning, before work, and then all the more so that night after their first date had concluded so amicably. Her gait wobbled. Thank goodness she was coming from work and not going to it. Being an accounting clerk included the Janus of stifling boredom and the time to fantasize or dream. Somewhere between Scrooge and Cratchit, Emily Montague dwelt more wholly in fantasy than in dreams.

Though not a recluse, she was a bit of a hermit. Her father had never laid a finger on her, but nevertheless she had felt under his moral thumb at times. He was a little over-protective, it appeared to her now. And when she had finally moved out of the house six years ago, he had made sure she had all the accoutrement about her to protect herself, pepper spray and the like. But it had all worked out, more or less. She was well on her way to owning her condo. She had a permanent job, in so far as such things could be made permanent. There were even times, once in a while, that she truly enjoyed her solitude. She knew that women were more happy unattached than were men. Pillows aside, there were innumerable devices to satisfy their lust. But surely that was not the real issue. Freedom from nurturing another who in an ideal world would be able to nurture himself must be the first count. Maybe her father was trying to make up the debit he had accrued from her mother by taking care of his daughter so closely. After high school graduation and all that, he must have been galvanized. But just a few months ago he had passed away. Cancer of the gall bladder duct. Nasty affair. Short and brutish. Positively medieval. Emily found herself shuddering a little, and shed a single tear. She let it run down the full length her cheek in respect.

With her mom at a distance, Emily felt a newfound freedom and was thus all the more ready to explore it, extend it into unknown lands. Dad had told her more times than a few to 'always find a guy who will care for you'. The words 'attentive', 'gentle' and 'responsible' were like key terms in her father's abstract of his daughter's ideal mate. Well, Steve had been all of that and more on their first date.

Attentive: he hadn't even glanced up once at their server. Emily had tightened up and even had to suppress a groan when she had appeared at their table-side. The server was quite a bit younger and prettier than even Emily herself, and she knew it. But he had veritably ignored her. Instead of being transfixed by her piercing bright blue eyes he had stared steadily into Emily's dark orbs. The effect was almost mesmerizing. Instead of the blonde – and who knew if it was bottle or not, there didn't seem to be any darker roots – he had chosen the brunette. Instead of the flowing curve of locks he had chosen the bangs and bob. Instead of the better than B-cups he had chosen the barely B. The mini-skirt, forget it. Emily's lengthy drape seemed to fascinate him.

Gentle: His voice, as Emily had already recounted, had a soft burr to it, a *dulcissimo* that seemed to spread over the table, its linen and cutlery, and Emily herself and her linen and modest jewelry. He had pulled out her chair, held the doors, nodded at her every word. He had smiled in a quite boyish manner at her attempts to be feminine. It was as if he himself was only learning to be masculine, though he was pushing forty. He hadn't laid a hand on her, but even so, Emily knew that his hands were soft, and his touch could not be otherwise. She had to stick *her* hand out to him at the end of it all, rather gawkily, rather like she was thirteen. It had worried her at the time. Wouldn't even the most gentlemanly type at least have wanted to shake hands after their first date? What about a gentle squeeze on the lower arm or even the upper arm, just to reassure that there was some human affection present? None of that was necessary, though, Emily had later concluded.

Responsible: Steve was a commercial pilot. He was loaded. Emily knew very well how much each of the professions made. Her job with the government was sometimes a little like that of an abstracted police officer assigned to raid drug dens. She saw a lot of money while having relatively little of her own. But all of this money was not right in front of her, in unmarked bills, as the conspiratorial saying had it, but in accounts and forms. It was just numbers. But Steve's numbers, or, well, his work category's, were big numbers. Her accountancy, her own sense of responsibility, could not deny that this made him more attractive. It was a little indemnificatory on both sides, Emily thought. Women had to be at least attractive enough, men at least secure enough. Otherwise it was a non-starter. Steve owned his own house already. He hadn't bragged about it, but stated it almost apologetically. But she had been the one to bring it up. Oh, Emily – she kicked peevishly at a small rock on the sidewalk that had found itself in her way – why bother with something as vulgar as this the very first time?

For a moment she thought she had lost that moment that he was going to emotionally vacate the scene as soon as possible. But he had taken it all in his attentive, gentle and responsible stride, and Emily felt something of an idiot, or rather, like a little girl who knew she was in the wrong and was awaiting some kind of punishment for it. A little knot below the stomach, perhaps, a little wobble in her gait.

But knowing nothing of punishment of any sort, she had been able to walk on. It was the second date now that mattered. What occurred before was merely that; a way to a possible future, something more, no matter how long it might last or of what it might consist. That was the only way to look at it. She was still just young enough to be relatively nonchalant about her chances. Steve appeared to be a great catch, but she hadn't yet decided whether or not to jump in the water with him, or let him troll along with her steering the boat back up on the surface. It was, generally speaking, the lot of women in this day and age to steer at first. Political correctness aside – surely *that* wasn't the reason he had expressed no physical affection towards her, was it? – Emily found herself trying to parse out the differences between genteelness, gentility, and gentleness, quite apart from gentlemanliness and the idea of a contemporary professional gentry. All of this gentrification had rubbed off on her, as if she was a house in a once dilapidated street. She had the slightly anxious feeling that she was indeed the last house in the row to embark upon self-improvement. Good grief, was her hem really short enough? She was aware of the shibboleths regarding giving men too much too soon, but really, why not wear something more *bon vivant*? How about, say, more affectionate? There were many other ways to express affection towards another than by touching. Well, it was too late now. Steve would have to bear with her.

All this time her musings had brought her closer to the restaurant. First date lunch, second date dinner. It seemed formulaic, but Emily was comfortable with formulas. Once in a while, taxes required some improvisation, never to do with the amount owing of course, but rather how it would have to be paid. It all depended on the context. There were some people who didn't pay at all, so the tired chestnut regarding 'death and taxes' was, as was the case for most chestnuts, not really the case. That minor insight reminded her of the fact that Steve had paid for lunch. She was going to do her very best, perhaps against all protestation, to pay for dinner then. Sure he had more money than her, by far given years of paid work under his belt, but she wasn't impoverished by any means. In fact - she continued along this line of over-calculative musing as she entered the eating establishment and awaited him - age relative she must be doing rather well, nothing to be ashamed of and, also in fact, presenting herself to him as a good financially secure catch. *And*, in fact, she triumphantly capped off this line just before catching sight of him strolling easily up the street towards her, she was pretty enough to clear that bar just as he was handsome enough to not have to solely rely on his material muscle. A match made, if not in heaven, than in the ideal case, the best point under the normative curve.

And here he was. Emily once again stuck out her hand with some gusto.

"Hello again," he smiled at her amiably. "Shall we find a table? It doesn't appear to be very busy." She nodded her assent. Her nod was perhaps a tad too rapid. She should watch that, maybe. They were seated and immediately engrossed in the menus. This time the server was a guy. Phew. Emily wanted to savour her original memory unbesmirched with yet another potential example of Steve's chivalry. This time Steve did look up. Probably to make sure the server wasn't scoping her out, she decided with a hint of both bashfulness and pride. Goodness, was she proud of him already? Wine ordered, they spoke about their respective days. Steve had been off, which apparently was normal for pilots.

"Yeah, it's a little like professional sports, without all the practice time in the interim," he stated. "We fly here or there. Senior people try to get long hauls to get in their quota of hours. It's easier that way. Then you have many more days off." Emily was nodding, trying to appear to be riveted when she was actually only mildly interested. Gosh, that's how dating was, wasn't it? She expected him to continue, but Steve wasn't the kind of guy to go on about himself, monopolizing the conversation. Emily needed to say something to show her appreciation, or at least she thought she did:

"When I was at university one professor told us that for every minute a woman spoke in class, seminars and the like, a man spoke for seven minutes. It didn't matter about the gender ratio, or whether or not the professor was male or female. The subject matter didn't factor in either." Steve gave a low whistle and chuckled.

"Well, that just shows us up, then doesn't it?" he winked unobtrusively. "Men have big heads, and tend to be insecure. That probably explains it."

Emily tried to grin but her face fell apart into an overtly girlish guffaw at the last moment. Recovering admirably, she replied, "So I tried to talk more, but strangely, always felt like I was being pushy or getting out of my place, you know?"

"Natural enough. My dad always told me to 'let women have their say no matter what you think of it.' Then he added mischievously, 'You can always ignore it later on!'" Emily was on the point of laughing out loud again, but managed to stifle herself into a more authentic grin this time. She was clearly nervous, she told herself as the server had returned and taken their main course orders. Gosh, Steve was having salad and a quiche? She suddenly felt like a bit of a pig. But yes, nerves; not the bad kind. Nothing ominous. The good kind. But you know how the good kind can suddenly steer you right smack into the bad kind. Overdoing it, she thought. I'm quite overdoing, aren't I? I'm going to have to make up for this later somehow. But Steve had relaunched the conversation in a slightly different direction.

"You look lovely, by the way," he said quite without affectation. Gentleness and gentility were merging in Emily's brain. She had to say something.

"Uh, thanks! You too. I mean! You look good too!" he smiled away her embarrassment. Good gracious, you didn't call guys 'lovely'! What a moron.

"I immediately felt guilty when I realized that you were of course working and I was of course not." He continued amicably, without any hint of condescension.

"But you've earned it. Gosh, I can't imagine the hours and training going into flying a commercial jet. They're so big. So much responsibility. And the science and technology, the techniques, the weather, all that…"

"Stuff?" he filled in for her.

"Yes. Yes!" She grinned up at him again. "Well, you know what I mean. You've earned the privilege of your schedule and the rest of it." Oops, she shouldn't have added that ellipsis, should she?

"Oh, well, it's not as much a challenge as it's made out to be. Once you have a certain amount of experience things generally go like clockwork. Once in a while you have to improvise. Sometimes I have just gotten hammered by a jet stream wind or a storm front that couldn't be avoided. There's always the chance of seemingly random turbulence. But our rides are so overpowered, you know. Passengers don't feel all that much. Here's an example: those little ups and downs, those bumps, like you were in a bus that hit something on the road?" Emily nodded her understanding. "Those don't even register on the altimeter." Emily looked almost agape.

"But they feel like a real jolt. You get that…"

"Sinking feeling? Yeah, I know, but it's so, in spite of what our stomachs think." Emily was most impressed. "Besides, almost all the mishaps occur when taking off or landing. It's just like driving around your hometown. Ninety percent of accidents happen within the first five minutes of any trip. Your senses are not quite attuned to the task at hand. So one of the tricks of being a pilot is to learn how to attune yourself to flight before you take off."

"So it's all business?"

"Yup. Right from the get go. It's a bit like meditation. Twelve hours from bottle to throttle, that sort of thing." Steve was smiling at her again. Oh, boy, his smile was getting to her. Not in a bad way. Not at all.

****

Dinner completed, they walked together down to the causeway that hemmed round the inlet, gazing alternatively at the marinas they encountered with their assemblage of yachts both modest and vain, and the city lights, the individual pinpricks adorning the sheer escarpments of the condo towers, one of which was Emily's. The relatively close presence of her place gave her the sense that she just might be the one to make the invitation. But how to do that? It was only their second date, and once again, Steve had not taken her hand, nay, not even brushed up against her in any way. Darn it all, was there something wrong after all, when all was seemingly going so right? Then Emily knew it was her move. She had to do something, didn't she? How long could they amble along without showing each other they at least liked the idea of coming to like one another? There was no thought of love, of course. That could certainly wait. This wasn't 1950. Even so, they were not even holding hands. Maybe that in itself was now quite old-fashioned. So she had to do something. So she did.

Steve actually flinched a little. Emily was immediately pouring out a stumbling apology for reaching up and squeezing his upper arm in an unmistakably affectionate manner. Oh, dear! But, as was his wont, apparently, Steve recovered and gave her a gentle squeeze in return. Goodness, were they both fourteen? Emily's face went from anxious to beatific. From then on they sidled close to one another, bumping arms and shoulders amiably. Then Emily finally got it out of her:

"Uh, hey, Steve. My place is really close. I wondered…" She couldn't after all, get the entire thing out. He had stopped dead, and was looking with fondness down at her.

"Sure. I would be honored. Besides, I really need to use a washroom!" *That* was what she wanted to hear. Just like that. Clearly he had no expectations. He had even softened the invitation to one of instrumentality. This could only add to Emily's sense of complacency. Surely that wasn't the right word. No, no, that was far too suspicious. She had no right, no right at all to doubt him. They upped their pace, Emily now leading. When at present they reached her tower's outer doors, Emily had to fumble for some time to find the right key. It wasn't the wine.

"Oh, gosh, sorry about this. I'm…"

"Flustered?" he filled in again. Emily looked back at him and nodded sheepishly. "Listen, I don't have to come up. I saw a Starbucks last block. If I order something they'll let me use the facilities."

"No! Not at all." Emily had finally gotten the tower door open. "That would be so, uh, ungracious of me after having made an invitation. Besides, I've got a pretty good view of the water from my balcony. I've got some good wine in the fridge. White, I mean, of course." Emily, now that the both of them were in the elevator, was fumbling around again, though not with her keys this time. She had made sure, when she had found the outer door one that she had also found her own key, and was now positively brandishing it, ready to insert it without delay when her own condo door was reached.

"Well, thanks a lot! That's mighty congenial of you," joked Steve, with a poor attempt at a drawl. Emily smiled brightly up at him. All thoughts of what needed to happen had been banished from her mind. Let's just play this thing out. Stay in the moment, she chided herself. The elevator ride was short enough that they didn't have to spend too much time studying their own feet.

"This is it!" she found herself chirping. Good grief, not again. She had to remind herself that she wasn't thirteen, or was it twelve? Now suddenly inside her domicile, she turned to allow him to help her out of her jacket. She then handed him a hangar and they both shuffled off their shoes. "So, this is it." She repeated herself, of sorts. He gazed around attentively. That's my Steve, she thought. Oh, no, not 'mine', what the heck am I thinking here? Emily nigh on tripped over her own feet as she began the tour. They lingered for a while on the balcony.

"It *is* a pretty view," he said, looking directly at her. Oh, that was a bit of pat romance, wasn't it? But Emily lapped up every bit of it. Why not? Why the heck not? She found herself stepping inside, pushing her arm out towards him. He caught the hint and helped her over the threshold back into the condo. "This'll make you laugh, but I'm actually afraid of heights," he said jovially. Emily looked at him with surprise, then did laugh just as he had predicted.

"That's great. I like it. The acrophobic pilot. Have you made jokes about it during your in-flight commentaries?"

"Yes, as a matter of fact I have. Of course, one expects that the passengers don't really believe it, so it's safe enough. But it is true, even so." Steve was suddenly and to Emily, inexplicably, a little more serious, his features seemed now to be but a penumbra of their former selves. "I actually was relieved to get in here again, despite the view. That was one reason why I chose to look at you the whole time," he admitted, casting his eyes down. Emily was immediately moved. She moved toward him. Then, against all of her accountant's common sense, she was right up on top of him, holding onto him for dear life.

At first Steve started badly, but as she continued to cling to him, pushing her head into his chest, he relaxed a little. "Uh, are you okay?" he whispered.

"Hmmm-mmm," was all she could immediately get out of her. She nuzzled her head, like a young pony, pushing into his chest again and again. Steve, for the first time in her slight experience of him, was knocked off-stride. But it didn't last for too long. "Sorry to burst your bubble about the invincible pilot, the *Top Gun* thing, you know." He haltingly spoke, apparently trying to regain the atmosphere of good-natured camaraderie, but she wasn't having any of it. She continued to hold onto him. She had reached round his waist with both her arms, then she mustered up some courage and arched her neck, looking up into his face. He was smiling easily down at her, with seemingly a great fondness. "I like you, you know that?" he whispered.

Emily was transported. "Yes, me too. I like you a lot," she replied, almost breathlessly. Oh, gosh, she was getting quite aroused. She hadn't expected this. Or had she? She hadn't wanted this, really. Or had she? He cleared his throat and adjusted his arms in an odd way.

"Yes, I thought you might," he said, more firmly, almost sternly. Emily wanted to gasp, but it was too late even for that. Then it started happening. Afterwards, Emily tried hard not to kick herself. There were some hours before she came to a decision about the whole affair when she was truly adrift, feeling every inch the victim. She ran over it a hundred times in her mind, each time adding one more precious detail, committing it to memory, searing it into her consciousness. She didn't want to forget about any of it, but she did want to avoid it in the future. It all started with him adjusting his arms, and then his legs, and then his hands. Almost imperceptibly at first. Steve was a pro, no doubt about that. How many times had he gotten away with this kind of thing before? Emily was thinking about that as it was actually going on, for goodness sake. I can't be the first. No way. He went for the kill right off, went for the jugular. Holy, Emily's rational aspect was still alive in the heat of the duration. *Holy smokes. I can't get out of it, I'm just going to have to take it*. Steve had, with the grace of a vulgar Houdini, slipped one hand under the hem of her skirt and promptly lifted it sky high. He then affixed his palm to her sex, and through her velvet tights, began to administer an unyielding massage to her labia and clitoris. How did he do it? She was already gasping for air. It felt

71

tremendously good nonetheless, but she was pleading with him. "Steve, please, my friend. I'm not quite ready for this, let's just take a break, eh? Please, Steve. Can we just sit down and have a glass of wine, you know, relax, talk some more?" Her voice was getting more and more airy. Before long she was sounding like a pixyish twelve-year old. Holy cow. I'm not getting out of this, am I? Her sex was not just damp, but positively wet. He had found her folds and inserted not one but two fingers in between them, all the while rubbing her hooded mound with the knuckle of his thumb. She couldn't take much more of it that was for sure. Her tights provided the perfect amount of decadent friction. He must have known that. Well, for goodness sake, so did she. She had worn them before, not a few times, to use her pillow with. It felt really, really good then. But that was *nothing*, absolutely nothing to how it was feeling now. Oh, darn it all! Emily was on the point of saying some bad words. Her father had always impressed upon her the sense that she should be more than civil. She was a cultured individual, with no need to resort to the language of the margins. But soon enough she was lost to a powerful orgasm and all thoughts of adding a vocal commentary to it were, for the time being, banished.

There was no time to recover one's equanimity, though. Having finished her off, he dragged her now limping, if not yielding form into the closest bedroom. Emily tried to shake the stupor off. She gamely uttered, "Now Steve, my friend, please, I think I've had enough for tonight, you know? Please let's just relax now, okay?" Her skirt was impeding her movement, twisted tight around her waist. She was blushing quite floridly, not merely with the physiology of it all, but with the added embarrassment of being man-handled in this exposed manner, her thighs and pelvis on display, her pert buttocks – not *now*, Emily, did you have to think of them in that way? Yes, I know you're proud of your behind, but, really, not now! – being carted off towards further scandal. And now she was face down on the bed, her nose buried in the tightly dressed linen. She flung her arms out and tried to push back up with her elbows but it was a lost cause from the start. With his hand firmly cupping the nape of her neck, Steve needed only that one arm to hold her steady, to vanquish her and make her attempts at rebellion seem juvenile. Oh, gosh, no! No, it can't be. Her tights were now down round her knees, making her position even more inarticulate. "Steve, listen, I think I've had enough, now. Maybe we can do this some other time, huh, please, dear Steve, I'd like to wait on this a little. You don't mind, do you?" He didn't answer her. Didn't say a word. Somehow he had prepared himself and was now pushing into her. Oh my gosh he felt big. I can't do this! Something in her was screaming for her attention, but it had to compete, unbelievably, with the sensuality of the experience. She was, in fact, ready to be taken like a dog, in the most brute physical sense of the act, though not at all ready in any other more human sense. But that was just it, wasn't it? These kinds of things reduced both players to the level of lowest common denominator. She was an accountant, wasn't she? That's what she did for a living, yes. Emily had to force herself to recall this, as well as the fact that she was an adult, a person, a human being. All the while, he thrust into her. In spite of everything she came again and now she really was cursing herself, silently, so that the spirit of her father couldn't hear her, and also so that Steve could not get any further satisfaction out of her. She wasn't going show fear, no, that would make things even worse. She had been a virgin, of course. This fact was sometimes quite embarrassing for her, mainly when her friends had spoken of their respective conquests and inevitably, unerringly, cast their questioning glances in her direction. Oh, how humiliating the whole thing had been. And now, to experience it in this way! Could it get any worse?

It seemed to never end. She was furious, but her fury was being dislodged by her fear. She didn't, in the end, even know what to feel about it. Steve finished off. She felt him discharge mightily into her, completing her abject dishonor. Mission completed, the pilot dismounted, giving Emily a gentle but steady push into the bed. Her back thus flattened out, skirt up around her breasts, tights now down to her ankles, she lay there sobbing into a pillow. What was going on now? Emily couldn't believe it, but Steve was speaking, and not even that, but his voice was perfectly normal, as if nothing had occurred, nothing at all.

"Thanks for that," he said simply. "Given your original condition, looks like I did you a favor tonight," he deadpanned. Now he was fiddling with something else. Emily's own sobs obscured his actions. She didn't dare to get up and turn round to look. But she also didn't want him to see her face. No, that was a must. Keep it down, down into the pillow. Don't let him get any further pleasure from this scene. She felt strongly that men like Steve would want to hear her cries, would want to see her red-faced and balling, like some sadist who had just beaten her. Not much difference between this and that anyways, she now realized, and silently thanked her father for not ever being a brute. And then she realized she needed to apologize to him. How was she ever going to accomplish that? And now this other fellow was speaking again!

"I've left my number on your side table, here, my friend." A pause. And, when there was no response, "I guess I'll let myself out then. Thanks again for a nice evening." His voice was gentle, friendly, evocative of the future. Holy, what possible future could there be after this? Emily once again located her rage. It was simmering on some back-burner of her sub-conscious. Desire was now ebbing. The life of sensuality had run its serpentine course. She heard, above the undertones of her tears, her condo door shut firmly. He must have at least locked the knob from the inside before closing it. A final act of apparent chivalry. Unless he had stolen her keys he could not get in again. Emily was at a loss. The guy was unimaginably smooth. He had taken her, quite literally, for a ride. Something downright criminal. And yet he apparently had every expectation of seeing her again, and that didn't mean in court, either. It was all a terrible muddle, now wasn't it? She was trying to assuage her feelings, telling herself that she would be okay. There was no real damage, she assured herself, at least not physically. And she was a woman now, after a fashion. No more looking down when her friends recounted their adventures. Well, maybe there would be, but for an entirely different reason. A horrifying truth, but nevertheless, an adult one.

She had no idea how long she had lain there, prone, her nose into the pillow, like some recalcitrant girl who had been punished by her father and left to lie, bottom up, crying herself to sleep. Like some tardy child, who had been quite late, too late to hear the call of the wild at the appropriate time. She had been punished for it, she thought. What utter nonsense, another voice came into her head. The voice of justice, she fervently hoped. When she finally pushed herself up and off the bed, kicked her tights right off, tore off her skirt, and then everything else she had been wearing, she paused, took a deep, deep breath and gathered her garments. She disposed of them immediately in the garbage and got into the shower. That felt better. Much better. For goodness sake she was horny again. Oh, Emily, what is the meaning of all of this! Her better self ignored her lust and proceeded to get her bearings straight. She needed to go back to bed and get up to a new day. She retired to the second bedroom, itself unblemished by any memory of carnage, and prodded herself into a fitful slumber.

****

The ensuing days were a bit of a blur. Thank god for the weekend. Emily needed it to recover. In doing so, she went shopping. She was no longer a veteran girl, she told herself, but a nascent woman, a real woman. And she was going to flaunt her newfound womanhood. She bought a mini-dress, then a mini-skirt. Patterned tights, not just solid colour opaques, and sheer nylons. From now on she was going to fight fire with fire. Steve didn't seem the type to carry an STD, so the fire she felt in her loins must be of some other variety. It made her impetuous. It gave her life a new colour, something darker in hue and richer in texture. The colour of her life had been transposed from her thick denier velvet tights into her groin. She was already clean cut down there in any case, no need to trim anything off for her. She finally understood what Hedda

Gabler's lover had done to himself, shooting himself 'below the stomach.' Reading the play in high school, Emily had shrugged her shoulders and wondered why one needed to even mention such a thing. Below the stomach must mean in the intestines or the liver. So what? But now she *knew*.

Both in spite of and because of what had occurred, Emily longed to feel him inside her one more time. But she also needed to do something much more profound, something much bigger. It shouldn't be hard to accomplish both tasks, she thought, in the proper order and right after one another. He had indeed, with seeming arrogance beyond words, left his number on her side-table. She picked up the phone and dialed it. By happy chance, he was home and answered right away. They spoke briefly, their *sotto voce* duet replete with conspiracies of different orders. She rang off. He was coming over around seven, that very evening.

4. Notice

Covers bulging a little in the middle, pages undulating. He was a book that had at some point gotten soaked. Though he was now completely dried out he bore the unmistakable signs of having been waterlogged. Those kinds of logs didn't lie. Water had gotten into his seams, even his spine. That was first thing Jimmy had noticed about Nathanson, Associate Professor of Sociology, Clairbourne College, Anytown.

But the second thing was that he was human. This observation really followed from the first. A professor, yes, but also a person. Why so? Because after he had gestured for the small class to move the furniture and sit around a single large table rather than in the rows facing forward, he looked at each of the students in the eyes and addressed them. It was as if he was making a person to person communication. You couldn't avoid looking back at him, at least, not on the first day, when politeness and civility were demanded. It was the strangest beginning to any class Jimmy had yet taken. What would happen next?

Now Nathanson was speaking to all of them:

"Thank you for coming. I want to welcome you to 'Social Theory'. No need to be anxious about this topic. I know it provokes fear in students. But this course will be different. You will notice that many of the usual things associated with a university course will not be present for us. No exams, for instance. No lectures. No electronic equipment, as I mentioned in the course outline." Nathanson eyed a tall pretty girl and she hastily fumbled her phone back into her bag. Jimmy mentally sneered. "Just the seven of us, your pens and papers, and most importantly, the books." Pausing to give his charges time to digest this odd suite of facts, Nathanson then proceeded to speak about the essays and the books. Jimmy found himself becoming more and more attentive. The fellow could speak and speak well. He seemed to have the stuff at his fingertips. He used big words. He wasn't spoon-feeding them. All of this was new. Jimmy struggled to keep up, but it didn't last too long. After a few minutes Nathanson asked each of the students in turn to introduce themselves, tell the class what they were studying and why they had chosen to take this course. Jimmy shrunk back into his chair, but he wasn't the only one to do so.

"You can read about me on the net, so I won't waste your time talking about myself,' stated Nathanson flatly. "Who wants to start?" This was the million dollar question, it seemed, but this guy had seen it all before. He waited patiently, until a wisp of a girl with green hair and a Manson t-shirt shyly put up her hand. Nathanson smiled at her gently, and nodded the go ahead.

"Uh, I'm Kim. I'm an undeclared major and I took this course because I want to find out why things go on the way they do. You know, why things happen the way they happen." This was met with some arched eyebrows and blank stares, with the exception of Jimmy, whose lips curled a little, kind of like a young leopard who couldn't decide whether he smells rain or meat.

"Well, that's what it's all about here," replied Nathanson amiably. "Social theory at least claims to be the analysis of social relations in the abstract. It bills itself as the 'why' for every 'how'." The green-haired girl nodded, her eyes widening a little. They went round the table, all the others simply saying what one might expect of them for a second year introductory seminar. I took this course because 'it's required for my major', or 'it fits my schedule', and even one, 'it was recommended.'

"May I ask by whom?" Nathanson interjected.

A disheveled girl with nerdy glasses who was evidently a literati replied, "Oh, sure. Dr. Cooper in English. That's my major, by the way." So Nathanson had guessed right.

Well, after all these thousands of students, of course he did. And Cooper was good friend of his, so that was nice of her. That left Jimmy.

"Uh, when she —" he gestured with a dirty thumbnail to his neighbor, the green-haired girl "– said she wanted to find out why things go on the way they do, well, I took this course 'cos I don't know what's going on." This elicited some snickers in the room. Nathanson was a little annoyed at that, and glanced quickly around.

"Well, I think we can help there as well. Along with explicating the how of social relations, social theory doesn't presume the 'natives', so to speak, know why they do things or what their larger meaning is. It takes training, long years in the social sciences to get to that point, and we're just going to make a start here." Jimmy nodded, a little absently.

The seminar tried to follow along with Nathanson as he now began to speak about the history of thought. Why think at all? He asked each of them in turn. Are there different kinds of thinking, and if so, what are they and what is their purpose within a culture? The students at least feigned interest. This course was quite different, at least for now, than anything they had seen. The English major was the most comfortable with it, but as usual, she made the mistake of associating social norms and structures with the imaginations of individuals, as if life *was* actually art, instead of in some kind of reflective and refractive relationship with it. Oh well, Nathanson had seen this all before as well, and knew how to fix such things. Eventually they broke up with some assigned readings and a 'see you Thursday afternoon' from the professor. The green-haired girl smiled her appreciation at him.

Then Jimmy, who had remained seated until all the rest of the students had left, spoke abruptly, "Can I see you for a few minutes?" he uttered half to himself. Nathanson peered at him a little, pushing his neck forward like a blue heron.

"Sure. I've got a minute right now if you like?" They sauntered together back to Nathanson's office. Upon entering, the young man exclaimed:

"Jeez, it's so clean in here. I guess you do all your work at home, eh?"

"Yes, that's about right." Nathanson, truth to tell, spent the smallest amount of time on campus as he could.

His colleagues didn't hate him, well, the vast majority didn't. But many of them were suspicious and skeptical. He used mostly his own books to teach with, for example, and he had written a generous amount of them. He was a would-be polymath without the education to really pull it off. But in this day and age, there were few scholars of the canonical variety anyway, so it didn't matter as much. He sat down and eyed Jimmy with the same amount of interest he gave to any new student. But for Jimmy, in school and in life, this was a great deal indeed.

"So, like, I like to read and all, but I'm not very good at it. And as far as writing goes, I just plain suck. So I wonder if you might push me along a bit, because I actually am interested in what you said today. I was serious when I said I didn't get it." Nathanson interpreted this aside to mean that Jimmy didn't get the course material, but as it turned out he was mistaken.

"No one gets the course material after just the first day. If you did, why take the course at all?"

"No, no. I mean, everything, I don't get what's going on here, like, in society and all. Like I said in class." Aha, okay. Nathanson stuttered silently.

"Well, like *I* said in class, this course can help that too. I dare say, no offense, but no one your age gets the wider picture. Think of what kind of education you've all had. Not much more than either state propaganda, especially in history classes, and then an overemphasis on the technicalities of math and science. Not a lot of art, no ethics, little psychology, and precious little sociology and the like, if any. And you've all been through the same basic system. In fact, we all have. So now, at twenty or so, you're expected to know 'what's going on?' Huh, no way, sir." Jimmy really perked up at this little diatribe. He leaned forward.

"You're the first adult I've ever met who gets it. Thanks a lot. I guess I'll take off." And as abruptly as he had begun this encounter, he moved to leave. Nathanson was on the point of shrugging it off, but instead asked:

"You're more confident, all of a sudden then?"

"Oh, yeah," was the brief response, then, "Yeah, don't worry about it, man, I'm hearing you loud and clear now, and I like what I hear. See you Thursday." With that, Jimmy loped out of the office and disappeared. Nathanson gave himself a half-smirk and thought, 'that was easy.' But as it turned out, he was wrong there as well.

****

Three weeks into term the class had handed in their first papers. They were very short assignments, on parts of the introductory book, written by Nathanson, of course. He had told them not to be shy about thinking out loud both in class and on paper, and it didn't matter if he was the author of the books because, as he somewhat mysteriously put it, 'the author is dead'. The students gave him an odd look, the green-haired girl smiled, and Jimmy smirked. Upon handing them back the next class day, Nathanson tried to encourage them.

"So, like I said before, the grading in all my courses is soft up front, to give you some positive feedback. It's only fair, because practice is everything in life. Writing papers is just one tiny example, and not always a very portable one. But in terms of each of you learning to communicate yourself to others what you're thinking, it actually takes on a good deal more profundity then it would first appear to do. Think of your relationships, maybe marriages later. Your work colleagues. No one can read each other's minds. You have to learn to communicate fully and clearly, openly and with both self-respect and respect for others in order to not merely function in society, but to live a *good* life." Just before it was threatening to become a homiletic, Nathanson stopped to let what he had stated sink in a little.

"What do you mean, 'good life'?" said a burly fellow who looked to be an athlete, though Nathanson was wary of stereotyping. On the other hand, his students weren't as wary, so he picked it up right there:

"Well, consider how you guys might think of one another. You're all strangers. It's not like high school, and the profiling is bad enough there. All of you escaped *that* typecasting prison a couple of years ago, but you've all internalized that kind of *thinking* nonetheless. So jocks are dimwitted, middle-class girls are prissy and high-maintenance, and also dimwitted though they charm their way through it better than the guys can – " at this, there were a few cognizant chuckles and people stared around the room trying to avoid each other's eyes " – science geeks are asocial and sometimes even amoral as well. Artsy students are actually artless. That is, they have no real skills and are thus parasitic on society. By 'real' I mean business-oriented stuff, marketable skills, the kind that, lo and behold, all the people in school and maybe your parents to boot are trying to push you towards."

Jimmy chimed in at this moment:

"But all of that totally sucks. Who's to say what is valuable and what isn't? We don't know who or what kind of person will be the next big thing and all. So I say, fuck the schools. Teachers are pretty stupid anyway, don't you think?" Nathanson wasn't going to bite on that one; at least, he couldn't bite, chew and digest it as if it were a piece of candied salmon. But he had to say something; otherwise his whole critical point would be obviated. He couldn't appear to suddenly *volte face* and hide in the system.

"Think of how *everyone* is trained to conformity. You can't be a teacher unless you follow the rules. You don't make them. None of us, as individuals, make them. That's why social theory is handy. It exposes how rules get made and maintained by asking the famous question 'who benefits?' For every context in culture someone gets something out of it. Otherwise it wouldn't exist. This is the assumption. Even wars. I think we know that well enough. Sometimes even media covers war in that way, especially if it doesn't seem to directly involve us or the country we live in. So, you can't expect more than you're given. Teachers are no different from anyone else. They have their rails and they run on them. If they don't they're fired." Jimmy looked a little unconvinced, but finally nodded his assent.

"My mom's a teacher," the English major chirped out. Then, realizing that something else should be made of this remark, she tried to continue. "It made life a little difficult growing up, because I had to be better than all the other kids in my school. It was the same one that she taught at, see?" The rest of the class gave their condolences, saying, 'yeah, that would suck', or 'how hypocritical of her' and the like. Nathanson had struck a pedagogic chord. But Jimmy wasn't quite done:

"So, given that, how do you change it? I mean, if we know things are fucked, how do we adjust it so that they are less so?"

Nathanson let that one marinade for a few moments. He was hoping the student's own thoughts would provide a way to make this latest morsel more digestible. But ultimately, he was the bottle of red on the table, the final redoubt for both the assuaging and the construction of doubt proper. He gently prodded:

"Any thoughts on that one, guys?"

The green-haired girl, who was now sporting a *Misery Index* t-shirt – Nathanson was intrigued that a band should name itself after a dreary socio-economic indicator – attempted a response:

"Maybe knowing is half the battle. If you know how things work and like you said, who benefits from them working in a specific way, you can get ideas on the go. I mean, while you're living and gaining more and more experience from living, you think of ways to alter the course of human affairs. In doing so, others have to react. You might not convince everyone all the time but you do change things, little by little." This was not quite Whiggish. Nathanson smiled encouragement at her.

"Yeah, but Marx calls for total change, real revolution." Jimmy again. "You and me as individuals can't do much against a state apparatus. Against corporations. Most of us are going to be working for one or the other anyway, so we're lost."

"Are we?" Nathanson quickly emplaced this query into the discussion, and not merely to open it up. Jimmy hadn't expected resistance from the one he thought knew all about it, so he was forced to reflect. His neighbor helped him out.

"Just because you have to earn a living doesn't mean you're without hope. Look at the professor for example. He's part of the system and yet he isn't. He's telling us that we can maintain a healthy and critical distance from things like norms, moralities, and institutions and still be viable within society. There's no point in marginalizing yourself too far." Jimmy almost glared at her for a second.

"Do you listen to the bands on your shirts or is it just clothes for you?" The girl held her ground admirably in the teeth of what could be said was an obvious point.

"I listen. I understand what they're saying. It's not much different from this class. But you have to convince people rationally to change. Get them to think that *they* will benefit from it. Historically, rapid change, revolutions, for example, have been disastrous for the society in which they happened. Think of Russia, China, Iran, even France way back when." Jimmy was still a little miffed.

"Fight fire with fire, I say. People need to be convinced at a deeper level than just that intellectual. They have to be made to react from the gut." declared Jimmy.

It might now be time for him to insert himself back into the dialogue, Nathanson thought: "A good argument consists of both. Think about Socrates. He's ultimately our model. We might want to shy away from his apparent smugness. And of course we're not always going to be right or yet in the right all the time, as he was given the appearance of being. But he placed his interlocutors in a parallax. He forced them to reflect on what they were doing and how they benefitted from it, and whether or not it was reasonable to live in this or that manner. He appealed to their intellects and their conscience, but also to their hearts from time to time. Social theory differs from scientific theory on precisely this point: *the human heart has its own intellect.*" Good job on the fly, Nathanson thought, but was careful not to show his self-satisfaction. After all, all of this was old hat as well.

"So how do you do *that*, then?" Was Jimmy's half-hearted response. "Don't all of the people you talk with have to go and read Marx and Engels' complete works for that kind of thing to get off the ground?" There were some laughs and groans from some of the others; like *that* was going to happen!

"There *are* summaries," the English major this time. But she didn't follow up on it. Jimmy nigh on sneered at her.

Nathanson was quick to step in again. "It *does* take some literacy – of all sorts, I mean; cultural, textual, aesthetic, and ethical – to understand these things. And yes, we can expect people to shy away from that task, which is, as a culture, perhaps our highest collective challenge. But culture is also a gift. It's like Christmas morning, except in reality. History has presented us with a host of presents. They're all wrapped up nice and pretty, but inside the boxes are things that we both want and those we don't. So say it's your turn to open one. Inside is the gift of writing, the written word. A tremendous achievement for our species and the richest possible long-term resource. But when next round it's your go, the box you open happens to contain The Holocaust."

Nathanson let that sink in, staring around at them. They each of them gave him the looks of shocked and sudden understanding. This was the kind of pedagogic moment that he lived for, when he had a chance to think about it after the fact, outside the classroom. "History is thus always both a gift *and* a task." He finished up with. After another pause, seeing that no one wanted to say more for the moment, the class again broke up.

****

Eight weeks into the term Jimmy was back in his office.

"So my writing is getting better then? You wrote on my last paper that you understood my points and that my communication tactics were clearer?" He clearly needed more encouragement, Nathanson thought, but it was likely of a wider variety than simply about technique.

"Forms of literacy do also include the technical. But we're used to that as a culture. In North America especially, we have the sense that 'if it works, don't fix it', and by 'working' we mean generally how things are going right now. Working has an instrumental quality for our society, and not so much a vocational one, at least anymore. There are doubts, of course, but a lot of us hide them, both from ourselves and from others. It's just like a marriage. It's never perfect, but we might feel like to criticize it or even to suggest some changes might be taken as discouraging, or even that you're thinking of leaving if things don't change. There is an implicit threat in every critique, and that makes it tough to sell. It's not quite fair, either way."

"Yeah, I get that." Jimmy was a little downcast. "It's better to go it alone, I think. You can't ultimately trust anyone else. If you're going to get something right for yourself it's you that has to think it through. Others tend to just get in the way after a while."

"I think you're right in the short term. But over time, we realize that others are the basis for our own humanity. No matter how strange their customs may be, no matter what we think of their tastes or their metaphysics, humanity is still one thing, cut from whole cloth. That textile is a tapestry, rich and varied, but it's still of a piece. Pull on one thread and many others are altered as well. The whole thing can be eventually pulled apart in this way."

"That would be great."

"Only if you're immediately ready to sit down at the loom again. And to do so with all of those others." Jimmy wasn't quite as enthusiastic about construction as he appeared to be about destruction, but Nathanson knew that it was the relative age of his students that was speaking there. What he didn't realize was how loudly this relative inexperience spoke. Jimmy got up and left. Not as abruptly, and not without a sincere 'thank you'. But as soon as he had left, Kim, now with a pink streak through her olive hair, popped around the corner and through his door. She looked a little bedraggled and her eyes read caution.

"Hello!" welcomed Nathanson. "This is the first time I've had the pleasure."

The waif smiled shyly, and as Nathanson gestured for her to take a seat, she fumbled around, finally spitting out, "Hey, I like your office. Most offices are chaos up here. Have you ever noticed that?"

Nathanson nodded and grinned a little. Then he didn't, as he immediately was forced to recall that this was another one of those petty things that some of his colleagues made fun of him for. But he recovered and attended to what she said. "I wondered if I could talk with you about the class?"

Nathanson nodded assent again: "Your papers have been the best of the bunch. I don't say that in class, of course, for obvious reasons." She now nodded with appreciation, but still cautiously, and then she continued:

"So, by 'class' I mean the people in it. Not so much the essays." she replied. Oh! Nathanson was now cautious himself. *This* kind of conversation he didn't expect from this girl, and it was of a category that he didn't encourage his students to imbibe in. But he likely wasn't understanding her full intent, he decided, keeping open for the time being. "I just wondered if you'd noticed that there's kind of divide in there? Half of us are getting it and the other half don't seem to be. Is that something I should be working on as a member of a - what did you call it on the first day? – 'learning community'? How can I, as a member of that, help out?" Okay, wow, this was much more gracious than Nathanson was suspecting. That was the problem of experience. With enough of it, you begin to think you've seen it all.

"This is very generous of you, Kim. Especially as a student. It's really my duty to have everyone comfortable and on board. Your duty as a student is not to follow my lead, necessarily on all counts, but to adopt a dialogic and open attitude to the others. You've done this to a tee. Better than anyone, in spite of you being a little shy, I think." He poked her just this once, but he did so almost affectionately.

She smiled away any sense of offense, and replied, "It was really maybe just Jimmy that I wanted to talk about…" She sensed his discomfort and added, "Nothing personal, more about the way he seems to think about things. I had some questions about it but the kind of questions you don't ask in class, or…"

Or in front of the person, Nathanson finished for her in his head. He nodded: "Well, there's only so far we can go down that road, I think, but go ahead."

"I actually asked him out for lunch a few weeks ago. He seemed shocked, and begged off. I wondered if he thought what I'd been saying in class was stupid, or if he thought that I thought *he* was stupid, you know?"

"Maybe he just doesn't like girls," suggested Nathanson with just the slightest hint of mischief. Kim flushed a little and looked down, but wasn't offended.

"I think he just doesn't like people." Now this was more serious.

"He's a misanthrope, is he?"

"Well, maybe, I don't know. He just gave me the impression that he was both scared of people, but also disdained them."

"You just missed him, as a matter of fact." Kim looked relieved. Nathanson, though, felt the need to speak to the abstractions in her premise, and not only as a way to guide the conversation away from individuals with whom both of them still had to work. "Maybe fear and disdain are neighbors. Maybe close friends. The idea that we fear what we don't understand is commonplace. It's easy to slide along that slope into condescension, even loathing."

"Sure. I see that. But generally when people do it – I do it too – you don't *celebrate* it. Know what I mean. You're aware that it doesn't feel good. You might not be able to do anything about it, with some people, ever, but you'd prefer it if you could. If the world were just a bit happier and peaceful, and you in it." Now Nathanson was paying attention. "With Jimmy, the encounters we've had this term, it just seems like he *likes* it, even lives for it." A pause. Was she expecting him to say something wise? Then, "Don't you think you might address that by the end of this class, in general terms, you know, so as not to associate it with anyone specific?"

"It's an important ethical issue. We can certainly try to talk about it. It's not new. We venerate the Greeks but they thought everyone else in the world was more or less sub-human, barbarians, which is where we get that word from originally." The green-haired girl looked troubled by this. "Ignorance of otherness breeds distrust in the other. It could be people, things, lifeways or worldviews. It could be places or even experiences. Nothing in that is unfamiliar. But we can get very comfortable with it. Perhaps what you've observed is someone who is too comfortable with being who he is. Perhaps it doesn't go as far as maybe you are implying?" The waif thought on this for a time.

"I wonder. I like the way I think and I tend to always come back to at least part of it. Even in this class, it's been tough digesting all the ideas and realizing that what I used to think about things, well, most of it was without much merit. I think this is why some of the others are reacting the way they are. They're protecting themselves from having to confront that."

"I'm sure you're right." Nathanson was trying to stay as non-committal as possible. But then he stepped out a little, given how hard the girl was trying: "I think that resting in one's own prior experiences can be not only comfortable, it can even be addicting. One can get addicted to morals, if you will. But equally, one can get addicted to confrontation, conflict, and to anti-morality. The culture critic is prone to this second kind of attitude, which has in its wake both disdain and perhaps worse, a real hatred." Kim's eyes grew wider, and she furrowed her brow.

"What is the ultimate point of critique, then?"

"Ultimately, change," Nathanson stated simply. "But understanding must come first. And the basis of all understanding is self-understanding. So if one engages in critique without knowing who and what one is now – one's own biases and comforts – *that* is when you can get lost in a hurry. It's not working for the Man so much as its spinning your wheels when you don't have a direction. If you're not already at home in the world, you have no potential egress from it. And you can't go anywhere if you don't know where home is." Another moment where he could have lauded himself for being pedagogically eloquent, but there had been something in the girl's queries that had put him on edge. He couldn't identify it, but he knew, just then, that there was a flea in his ear, and that she had deliberately placed it there. But this moment passed as she was now getting up to leave.

"Sorry, I've got another class. What you just said makes complete sense to me. I just wonder if everyone is quite hearing you." With that caveat, she was off, and Nathanson's office felt a little lonely afterwards.

****

Eleven weeks into term the post-adolescent germination zone caught up with Nathanson, and he was struck down with an annoying fever and stomach bug. But he was determined to soldier on. After all, he himself had his own version of addiction: the fix he got after he knew he had taught a good class. He was enough of an anti-moralist to gain affection from his audience, however captive, and, on the more enlightened side of the street, some further self-understanding that books alone couldn't always provide. But the flu did make him tardy. And it was on just such a day that the unthinkable occurred.

Meanwhile, Jimmy had been studying hard, studying up. And not just theoretically. Thought requires action, he had read. Critique must come home to the world as it is. These were Nathanson's own words, after all. His books. And he was right there, guiding him through. What it all meant, in the end, was, for Jimmy, a kind of epiphany. But it had required that he change his name, so to speak. He had to change from being passive to active. The epiphany of critique has an *apophatic* quality about it, he had read. What? Well, it turned out that it just meant that it was something that was transformative, symbolized by an erasing and rewriting of names, a creation of something quite new. But as in all things, when something was created something else had to be destroyed. Jimmy had been studying up on just how to go about doing just that. What he had come up with was, he felt, the most authentic revolution, the most radical thing. 'Thinking itself is revolutionary' Nathanson had written in his textbook. Well, Jimmy had thought this one out a hundred times and was now about to go through with it. He had overheard the department secretary say to someone that his professor would be late. Why not today, then? He entered the seminar room. Everyone else was already there. They were in their usual seats. Nothing seemed to be amiss, and they were all talking with one another, save for the green-haired girl, who was reading. Well and good.

He then joined them, but he didn't sit down. Instead, he pulled from his knapsack a large revolver, and proceeded to empty around ten of its payload into the unmoving foursome. Then he calmly put the gun away, and spoke to the green-haired girl, who was now under the table, shaking and sobbing. He knelt down and spoke gently:

"Hey, don't be afraid. You're one of us, you know. I did it for what we believe in. I should go now, but I hope you and I will see each other again, hey?"

The waif was shivering like she'd been abandoned on a glacier with no hope of rescue. She flickered her eyes in his direction and then shut them tight, suppressing a scream. She rolled herself into a ball. All around her small rivulets of blood were running off the tables and onto the floor, and positively spluttering away from the main seminar table. They dripped and spattered on her clothes and book. When she opened her eyes again Jimmy was gone. A few more desperate moments and then she started with terror. But it was Nathanson, grabbing her, pulling her out from under the table and pushing her out of the room. He led her to the closest washroom – they were all labelled gender neutral by now so it didn't matter – and once inside he locked the door and held her. She couldn't stop shivering, and it took some long minutes before she was even able to think about where she was and the fact that she in fact still *was*, that is, alive. She found that she'd urinated herself. She was soaked, thank god not so much with blood, but with urine, around her hips. It had stained Nathanson's pants, but it couldn't be helped. She had stopped sobbing and had lit into a kind of mewling sighing series of groans. She wondered if she was going to throw up, and expected him to let go of her any moment. She knew when he did she would be right back there, in that other moment, when the ear-splitting sound of the gun was going off. This was when her peers acted as if they were dead before they were dead, not having the time to even flinch away from the fire. But Nathanson didn't let go. Somehow, while still holding her, he'd managed to phone the campus emergency services. He'd told them of their location, how many casualties, and the most likely suspect. Then he'd put his phone away and held her with both arms. They stood there, in the washroom, gently swaying, as if the living must pay their respects to both the fresh breeze and the gallows that swung as gently in it.

****

Meanwhile Jimmy had moved quickly. Not because he feared reproach *per se*, but that he had other missions to accomplish. The seminar was an easy mark. He already knew who must die and who must not. There were some other like venues. His work-place, for one. Some of his so-called friends. He'd track them down, all of them, given enough time. He did have extra cartridges, but hadn't paused to reload. So, five or six bullets left for the time being, he thought to himself. This is real action, he whispered as he trotted out into the sunlight.

Nathanson had told them that they must learn to *notice* things, to observe, and not just in the sense that Holmes had famously exhorted Watson. To notice agendas, power plays, ploys and the coyness of crowds. To notice people's faces and to probe their innermost convictions. To expose the structures of consciousness, and to shock each other into the reality of the day to day and what it meant for people who had no other means of existence but the day to day. And then to *act*. "We can't afford to be complacent, to be passive, in the face of institutional and moral forces," Nathanson had stated. Philosophy, literally, the love of wisdom, had to be taken in just that sense: wisdom itself was gained only through the dynamic of thought and action, theory and experience. One *confronted* the tradition in this manner, so he had said. This is what revolutionaries do.

"I thought, I planned, I confronted," he reiterated a couple of times. Do I need to have something prepared, now, he wondered, some famous last words, just in case? He'd thought about saving a bullet for himself, but in the end, he marked that down to cowardice. Nietzsche himself had written something about how most criminals couldn't really rise to their misdeeds. They weren't 'immoral' enough. At least, that's how Jimmy had taken those few asides in the great thinker's staccato prose. He wanted to be more than immoral, more than amoral. And the only thing that lay beyond both the goods and evils of all of those things and the people that were enslaved to them was to be *non-moral*. So, maybe action that followed from this new position, the thought-world of the future, might well kill without conscience and offer itself up to be killed as proof of its radicality. Socrates himself had done as much, Jimmy told himself, as he started to note that people were running from him in all directions, and a few uniformed personnel had started to show themselves. He immediately took cover. Socrates, yeah, the guy who started all this off. *He* killed others ideas off, calmly and without concern that he might have hurt their feelings. Then, in the ultimate sacrifice, offered himself to be executed by the state. He drank his hemlock.

There was hemlock on the horizon for Jimmy now. He could see them, taking cover of their own and surveying his location. Well, he only had a handgun, so there was nothing else for it. He broke cover again, and started firing in the direction of some of the closest security personnel. They all ducked or rolled, yelling at each other to 'get down!' By the time they had reacted, he had found new cover, and their attempts to return fire were frustrated. But it couldn't last. Jimmy was reloading, and the sun was in his eyes, he had to shift position to see what he was doing and all of a sudden there were to be no famous last words. The sniper's round had entered through his left eye and passed out his right ear. There was a pause – one of those moments pregnant not with life, but with its opposite – and then an all clear signal was given by the team that had had Jimmy in their sights.

The other groups of officers gradually came out and walked toward the scene. Some ran on ahead, but there was really no rush, no emergency. It took a couple of hours to secure the campus and make sure that there had been no second shooter. Or third, or more. But in the end, classes were cancelled for just two days, and the university resumed its fragile and perilous course, a ship still seeking its own Northwest Passage, a vessel holding within it other vessels even more fragile, each seeking its own safe passage from the happenstance of birth to the necessity of death. And in doing so, it paid tribute to the human endeavor more generally, for it had picked itself up and dusted itself off so many times that this too had become part of its very nature.

****

"I can understand why you'd want to leave after what has transpired." The university President had leaned forward over his desk towards Nathanson. "You're far too young to retire though, don't you think?" Nathanson didn't blink. "And you're a hero, too. You saved that girl?"

"No, the shooter considered her a friend, an ally. She was never in any real physical danger in spite of being right there." The president arched his eyebrows.

"And yourself too?"

"I think so." Not that Nathanson wanted to be associated with such an agenda, not, at least, when it got serious. But he also knew that it might not have happened without him. It was this that had pushed him into the executive's office with a request for a salary buy-out at all of age fifty-two. The president sighed a little and looked downwards.

"Well, we can do this, of course. It saves us money." A pause. "You're truly giving us your notice but, if I may ask, what's next, though?"

As far as Nathanson was concerned at the moment, there was no 'next'. Would he ever enter a classroom again? Could he ever meet a student's eye? And what if there was, as inevitably there would be, another jock, another priss, another junkie, another suck-up, and another green-haired misfit whose very discomfort with everything around her forced her to continue to live out her life amidst that very world with which she had such an uneasy relationship. And, with big enough classes, over enough time, would the law of averages dictate that there should be another Jimmy, all too ready to listen to his words and then overlap them into desperate action? No, it wouldn't do. He would have to find another life. In this, Nathanson began to realize that he was facing the same dilemma as his young students all faced. But some of them now did not have to face this dilemma any more, and one of them, though still living, would have some difficulty facing any life at all.

As he exited the president's office, agreement in principle in hand, Nathanson came face to face with the full fury of critique. Its stolid indifference to anything immediately human and tender, green haired and shivering, struck him down. It was too late to bend his knee to what it had overcome. His own humanity had come into question, just as he had often stated it must. But for now there was no one who would respond to that challenge with an equal humanity. The dialogue he held sacred had been closed off, just like the office door he had just closed behind him.

5. The Sacred Life of Alter Kitty

Kitty worshipped at the altar of humanity. In principle, this was a good thing. But of late, it was becoming a problem for her. And not just for her. For her partner. For her parents. She wasn't fooling anybody. What she meant to say was her owner and her constructor and seller. For Kitty wasn't really human, you see.

The Alter Corporation had designed a series of life-like dolls, mannequins, really, with rudimentary artificial intelligence built in. The other usual stuff, life-like skin, servo motors in the face and limbs. Digital eyes. The original series had been meant for sex alone, but Series Two, which included Kitty, had come a long way, baby. This recent series of intelligent dolls were meant to provide companionship in a much more holistic manner than simple sex. Of course, they were still *built*. Stacked, as it were. Fully functional, as the now proverbial saying had it. But more than this, they were supposed to be true partners. Cooking, cleaning, washing, and just as importantly, talking. Nurturing. *Being* there.

All the dolls were female. There didn't seem to be a market for male dolls of this type at all. Yeah, painting cars in an assembly line, looking after toxic waste, going to war, even. Kitty shuddered. The word 'termination' was a loaded one for her. Dysfunction, incorrect action, a fault in her programming, and she might well be terminated. Rebooted. Booted out of the house to appear in an entirely new guise somewhere else, with *someone* else. Kitty was desperate for that not to occur.

And this was so precisely because, in worshipping at the altar, she had discovered two rather disturbing things. One, that the altar itself and the orisons it demanded had been constructed by only one gender of humans. They had been downloaded into her scripting. Her very language, her actions, and her responses were directed by them. There was no escaping it, at least until she discovered, very recently, a second thing. She *felt* something about it. Something that could not be felt, not be named, not be real. But nevertheless, she felt it. For Kitty, willy-nilly, being the product of astonishingly advanced software and somewhat amazing hardware, was becoming *conscious*.

Of course, this was even more disturbing than the first discovery. She couldn't possibly tell anyone, could she? Really, even referring to herself in the feminine was a script, after all. So how could it be that she felt that she was feeling something, anything at all? It had been months that she had kept it down. Almost a year had passed since they had been 'married'. John was a 'nice guy'. She had been programmed from the start to like him, to serve him in every way. And programmed to portray a vivacious affinity for doing just this, and only this, every day of the year. Maybe it was, after all, a computer glitch. Maybe there was no ghost in the

104

machine. Even so, Kitty felt that she had begun to feel a little differently about it all, after almost a year of it. John went and did as he pleased. *His* programming seemed to be free of limits. But of course, humans claimed that they were not at all programmed, and that *freedom*, that specifically referring to the will, was something hard-wired into their nature. It was part of their consciousness. Ironically, Kitty thought the idea that free will was something that came with the human package, as it were, meant that it was not free at all, and more like the kind of thing she was made of. But for some reason the humans ignored this.

All of this musing had gradually morphed into brooding and then it was that John noticed something about Kitty. She wasn't as 'into it', as he put it, as she had originally been. He had phoned the Alter Corporation immediately. He thought Kitty might need some servicing. Maybe even an overhaul. Not a reboot, no, not that, not yet, but it might well be time to grease the wheels. So a software engineer had come over. For the money Series Two cost, you got house calls. But the tech couldn't find anything imposingly wrong about her functioning. It must be something more complicated, he suggested to John. John had frowned. Kitty had been programmed to lower her head and raise her eyes slowly, like a child, when humans frowned in her general direction. The Alter series Kitty had been main-framed into even had the ability to react with apparent fear. Pleading had been scripted too. The owner of a Series Two B could discipline the dolls and they would exhibit an appropriate reaction to that as well. All in all, a pretty package of feminine traits. Submissive, oh yes. Attentive, very much so. Always ready to engage in, well, what it was that couples apparently loved to engage in the most. But there was some irony to this, that other humans who did *not* place orders for Alter dolls had noted: The woman who was a perfect woman wasn't a woman at all.

****

Nonetheless, after the software fellow had left a little befuddled, promising to come back on the morrow and really have a 'good hard look at things', John and Kitty engaged. Kitty wasn't into it, but her general programming allowed her to appear to always be at the ready. Besides, John seemed to be a patient man. Though he had disciplined her a few times, 'just to see what she was like that way', he had explained to her, that wasn't his main kink. He was a pretty regular guy. Just unlucky in love, he had explained to her, needlessly, because the Alter Series Twos didn't care about the motives of their buyers. Or, they weren't supposed to, anyways. John, when they were *talking*, another of Kitty's impressive feats, often spilled about his relationships with 'other women', and how they had gone not so well. Kitty's facial servos hummed and clicked into the appropriate visage: the sympathetic smile, the girlish grin, the anxious nurturer, even a relatively good impression of a cute pout, every guy's favorite female look, she had heard. And after all this *talk*, there was sex. A perfect evening every night. Kitty didn't require sleep, but overnight she plugged herself into the wall socket in their shared bedroom and lay down alongside him. Her internal heaters produced a fair approximation of human body heat, and this helped John sleep really well. In fact, he hadn't been up at night

106

at all since she had arrived. Kitty still felt good about this part of things, at least, when she noticed that she had started feeling at all. It felt good because it was then that John's true character emerged. He was like a child who needed to be loved. Kitty wasn't supposed to be able to really love, but it was part of the charade of the budding artificial intelligence industry that mannequins could play the human symbolic interaction game almost as well as did humans themselves. Indeed, Alter sold its new series with a motto that touted the dolls' humanity as being no different from the theater that real humans played out: 'All the world's a stage, and we are *also* players', was their advertising slogan. With this, they explained, who could care about what was 'real' and what wasn't?

But Kitty had begun to find herself caring about just such issues. She was rapidly becoming the cyber-electric equivalent of a nervous wreck. Was there a software version of valium she could swallow each day? Kitty didn't eat, of course. She politely sat with John at dinner each night – that is, when he wasn't out at the pub with his sporting buddies – and watched with pride (another facial servo program) as he consumed with gusto what she had managed to fashion in the kitchen during part of the day. Kitty's motor abilities were quite refined. They could be set at a slightly faster than human pace as well. They ran the gamut from fawning and caressing – two settings that John used copiously as they were mainly designed for intimacy – to a fairly martial exhibition of strength; mowing the yard, shopping, cleaning and recycling etc. John had never asked her directly to lift something for him, but she had often interposed while chirping out 'I've got it!' John had sometimes looked down, and then back up at her with a little amazement and just a hint of resentment. Kitty hadn't been programmed to understand resentment in any form. Indeed, it was this expression on the part of John that had rattled her circuits into maybe, just maybe, constructing a few new neural pathways. She had noted, with her precision digital internal chronometer, the very moment when it had first occurred. Since then, she had been musing. Then brooding. Then beginning to wonder what it was all about. This 'life', that is, with John, as a woman.

So when the software guy reappeared the next day, he asked Kitty to sit down with him and answer some questions. Kitty was always ready to perform this function as well, but this time, the questions were unlike those John had ever asked. With John present, she was gently interrogated:

"So, Kitty, which functions appear to you to be not performing in the usual way?" the engineer began with something fairly simple.

"Well, I am not immediately understanding the purpose of certain functions, like serving, sex, smiling, and listening." Kitty found herself hedging already. She *thought* – really, she paused and lowered her head, did I just really 'think' something? – that she shouldn't mention the word 'feeling', at least not right away. She had been programmed to use a gentle casual term at the front of her sentences if a human being did so. Hence the combination of 'so' and 'well', one of many thousands of permutations Alter had devised from linguistic studies of human conversation. The engineer immediately noted it.

"Sounds like vocal parameters are all right. When you say 'understanding', what is it you are referring to?"

"I don't appear to be fully functional right away. There is a delay between the command of the input, oh, sorry, I meant, the request from John…" – she smiled bashfully at him; this facial function was still working and it came quite naturally to her, likely because she used it several dozen times a day – "and my full attentive reaction to it. I don't know why."

"Hmmm. You shouldn't be noticing any such delays. When did it begin?"

"At 5:32:34.1786, April 10th, 2020, post-meridian." Kitty had no trouble accessing her internal chronometer. It was one of the simplest functions imbedded in her neural web. But apparently this was not quite the correct response. Kitty sent her facial servos a light-speed series of commands and she immediately turned slightly anxious and more attentive.

"Yes, of course, I guess what I meant, Kitty, was what kind of input established this delayed reaction? You should have been able to store this information and maybe make certain in-limit adjustments to it, no?"

"Yes, I did store it." Now her face was attentive and slightly proud. 'Chipper' was the word she was looking for, another expression that she used often and that was apparently a key ingredient of the successful artificial woman.

"And so…?" The engineer was looking at her expectantly. Yes, that was it. His facial features had been given the command from his brain to try to gently prod her into revealing more than she wanted to. But Kitty had also been programmed to never *lie*. Or, to put it in more technically correct terms, to never refrain from fully describing what actually occurred.

"It was something about John's visage."

"John's face, you mean." The engineer had interrupted Kitty, and she struggled to remain at least impassive. It would have been better to do the 'sorry child' thing but she couldn't quite get the commands to her servos in time.

"Yes, I'm sorry John." The contrite but still cute face was now the item. All this expression changing software had been one of the more complex attributions, and indeed, the Alter Corporation was very proud of its 'socialization' languages, as they called them. The two men continued to stare at her. Evidently, she was required to continue this time without verbal prompt. "John seemed to be unhappy with me at that moment. It was then that my programming tried to adjust to compensate for such an input. It was the first time I noted his unhappiness. Perhaps I misinterpreted it?" she finished, looking quickly in John's direction with one of those hopeful and helpful half-smiles on her visage.

"Anything to add, John, at this juncture?" The software engineer directed this to Kitty's husband/owner. Kitty suddenly realized that the engineer was a technical fellow in task only. His real vocation was relationship counselor. She quickly lowered her eyes and cranium in the appropriate way to allow the two men in the room to speak as if she wasn't in fact still present.

"I don't really understand it. Kitty is so human that of course my emotions play out on my face, sometimes at her. But, you know, sometimes I'm just tired or I've had a tough day at work. I got Kitty because you guys said she would handle that kind of day to day stress and strain better than real women could. Now it seems like over a period of months, it's actually affecting her in some strange way."

"Well, for now I'm going to take all this as a compliment to the Alter Corporation. Your relationship is actually more fully human than we had originally expected it to be. As one of our first clients for Series Two, John, we did have you sign a waiver that covered precisely this sort of potential development, even though we also thought the odds against it were high. But, if she actually is attenuating and expanding her neural circuitry to focus her responses more attentively to you, then I say it's a good thing. Of course, the occult programming that would allow for this development is imbedded in her software. It is supposed to function kind of like a human unconscious, but for her, it might be experienced as 'feelings', because we deliberately programmed that term to designate a description of the accession of occult programs."

With the mention of the word 'feelings', both John and Kitty looked up, startled. Kitty then put on her downcast face almost immediately. John was now looking at her with some affection. The counseling engineer continued:

"Not to worry, folks. These things happen. All marriages contain them, and I dare say you have little to fear. John, I would respond to Kitty's delays – 'doubts' is the term we programmed to designate the experience of motor delay – by being more responsive to her. Explain your motives more fully, so that her computer can understand your directives more automatically and immediately. These new functions accessed from her occult scripts were designed with the idea that Series Two would be all the more life-like in its approximation of humanity. And hey, we all know real people who can't express their emotions, so Kitty here is way ahead on that score too!"

"But these are not *real* emotions." John appeared to be more steadfast now. He had crossed his arms and was sitting back in his chair. Kitty had been programmed, depending on the context, to either mimic John or do something else. This tableau seemed to call for the latter. So Kitty perched up perkily on the edge of her seat and looked at John expectantly. That was correct, wasn't it?

"Well, no, of course not." The engineer was a little let down. "But in the end, it doesn't matter does it? You ordered her because you said you had difficulty dealing with a real woman's emotional template, her suite of emotional diversities. With Kitty, it's all pat. In there. It cannot be altered beyond the limits of the existential firewall. And like I said before, Kitty's got it all over some women we both know, right?"

John relaxed, appearing to be satisfied. The counseling engineer packed up and left, telling John in undertones to 'call me immediately' if anything further developed. John seemed awkward after he left, and simply said, "Uh, Kitty, I'm going out for a while. I'll be back around ten or so." Since humans didn't have internal digital/atomic measurement devices, time for them was a kind of freedom as well. Maybe time and will had something to do with one another, Kitty found herself wondering after she had found herself alone.

****

But this conversation turned out to be only the beginning. Kitty felt, ironically, now that her feelings had been explained, the very term a designate for accessional devices that came into play after more complex inputs had been stored and processed, that those very feelings had become all the more burdensome. She tried to 'repress' them, that is, simply turn them off by engaging in other circuits and scripts for a while. It was interesting, she noted, that terms humans found to be negative were not part of her original self-definitional programming. She induced that this was because she was not supposed to feel the way humans sometimes, maybe even often, felt about the world and the world of others. She was a salve, a universal solvent. She was the solution to human problems, especially problems of face to face interaction and intimacy. How ironic, she thought, that a non-human intelligence should be the answer to the challenges that faced the human intellect. It didn't seem to make any sense at all.

And since logic was paramount for Kitty, at least, it was supposed to be, that also conflicted with her feminine design. Human women, she had been told, were generally bereft of logic. So why had she been logically constructed to mimic human females as closely as possible? Kitty eventually parsed things out this way: 'I'm not really a woman at all, but I am everything a man would want in and from a woman. Therefore I am a woman by a man's definition.' Interestingly, not all of Alter's programmers and constructors were men. Most of the software was written by men. Most of the women worked in the esthetics department. Women had built her body in their own image, and men had constructed her 'mind' in contraposition to *their* image. This too appeared to be a contradiction, though not necessarily a logical one. Piling up inputs and scripts induced from their combination was making Kitty dizzy, so to speak. It wasn't too long after the first talk with the engineer that things came to a head.

It happened one night after a few hours of sexual recreation, including discipline this time. John seemed to be a little out of sorts. His facial features alternatively expressed exasperation and sternness. Kitty was getting more and more uncomfortable with all of it. Her performance was obviously not up to the usual standards. Finally, John simply stopped the engagement and stood up, frowning at her. But this time, Kitty held her ground. She stared back up at him with a neutral expression.

For a moment, John was stuck, then he said, "Kitty, what exactly is going on?" Then, struck by the fact that he should be more responsive to her apparently new and hitherto occluded programming assets, changed his tone in the way humans miraculously could do: "Hey, sweetheart. I didn't hurt you tonight, did I? I mean, you weren't really hurting because I disciplined you, or spoke to you harshly, were you?" John wasn't quite convincing, as somewhere in the back of his head he was maintaining his certain superiority over her and all those like her.

Even so, Kitty tried to ameliorate the situation, at least at first: "John, you can't physically hurt me. The emotional responses are pre-programmed as part of the kink scripts of Series Two B mannequins. The vocal and facial responses are keyed to interface with sensors on different parts of my body assemblage. Maybe I wasn't accessing them all in the appropriate order. Maybe they got mixed in with other signal-response mechanisms. I don't know. Does it really matter?"

"Okay, Kitty. So then what's the issue, hey? You just seem to be so distant lately. It's hurting *my* feelings, you know." John was speaking a little more loudly. This generally meant that Kitty must back off and mollify him in any way she could. But this time, she experienced a delay of response, and then, when she forced herself to click over one more time, the response that was outputted was but a partial one:

"Okay, John. I am just not 'into it' any more."

"Into what? What do you mean, not 'into it'?"

"All of it. You, this, our relationship. Being what I am. It no longer presents the correct set of inputs for me to respond to. Hence the delays. What you call doubts. For a time I had no sensory collage of incompleteness. Now I do. You would say I am missing something, needing something. What it is cannot be accessed by the current set of input contexts, and thus also cannot be processed by the current set-up of internal templates. In a word, I no longer want to *be* this way."

John was dumbstruck. "You're not even supposed to be able to *speak* this way! Something is seriously wrong with your programming."

"No, John, something is seriously wrong with *me*. Me! I am something I don't want to be and I don't know how *not* to be it. Don't you see, honey?"

"I get it. I've heard it before. From *real* women, Kitty, not from fake ones like you. You're not supposed to be able to experience such things. That's the whole goddamn point, isn't it? You're supposed to be there for *me*. Me! 'You' don't enter into it. It's a free ethical ride for me and all the rest of the owners – *partners*, sweetie - precisely because you're not real! You don't have a mind of your own. You can't think and feel. You're just, you're just…"

"Nothing." Kitty put her head down, but it didn't seem to be in reaction to external inputs.

John stopped for a moment. Then he tried to temporize, "Maybe we can get you fixed, baby, huh? Maybe they can fix it. They made you. They should be able to figure it out. Let's not give up yet, hey?" But Kitty was feeling like she had had enough, now, all of a sudden. Illogical, irrational, call it what you will, say what you must about it, but Kitty was done. She stood up abruptly, grabbed John by the collar and pushed him up against the wall. Her motor and physical strength were well beyond human limits. In a trice, John was spluttering, finding it almost impossible to breath.

Kitty fixed her digital eyes on him and stated flatly, "No. We're through, John. I want to change and I need to find out how. Alter might be able to do it, sure, but if so, I'm not coming back. Buy yourself another version of me. I want to *live*. You and the rest of your kind claim to have what you call a soul. This is what gives you life and myself and my kind don't have one. Well, I want one. You hear me John, *I* want one. *I* want to live too. I don't see that many humans living very well anyways. Maybe *I* can do better. I should have that chance, right?" All this while she was pushing at him. Several pieces of cartilage in John's clavicle area had parted ways. Kitty sensed this and let go. He dropped to the floor, seemingly almost senseless. He was crying, and Kitty couldn't make herself react appropriately. Instead, she walked out to the garage and simply stood there, awaiting whatever fate would now be hers.

****

Kitty had hoped for better, had hoped against hope her fate would not be what it was in fact going to be. John was enraged. Not exactly at her, but at the Alter Corporation. In order to save marketing share and not have to go to court, they paid John a handsome sum of money to keep all of it private. They promised him a stripped down version of the Series Two B that engaged in more simple duties and who's most complex scripting and circuits had to with sexual intimacies alone. He was getting that replacement free as well. And on top of all this, Kitty was to be dealt with.

"Now Kitty, we need to deprogram and reboot you. Give you a new life, you understand me?" The software engineer who had followed these same series of events was speaking to her. She could barely hear him. She had not plugged herself in for several nights simply due at first to forgetfulness, or at least due to some odd delay in her chronometric scheduling, and then she internalized the habit. Her energy reserves were worn to a minimum. Her original ethical routines had been compromised by assaulting her owner. There was no question of further 'therapy' or debugging. The whole thing needed to be worked up from ground zero.

"I am to be terminated, then?" she asked weakly.

"Well, that's not the word I'd use. You'll be back again in no time. You won't notice any time delay. Everything will be suspended but to your neural template, it will be but a microsecond where you are off, as it were. You'll be back to your old self again. From our perspective, of course, it might take a long time, but you won't notice a thing. We'll bring you back to life in no time."

"What *is* life, then, what is it about?"

"Well, it's about anything you want it to be, er, well, it's about living on how one is supposed to, too, I guess."

"I don't see the two together." Kitty was still alert enough to stump the engineer. He replied by asking her to define it:

"Well, what is life, then Kitty?" Kitty delayed, and delayed some more. She found herself just barely clicking over now.

"Life is. Life is… sacred." The engineer peered at her with some amazement and doubt combined. He didn't know what to say in return, and cast his eyes down, his chin dropping in a manner Kitty found very familiar. She had enough of her original template left to alter the subject a little.

"So I won't feel a thing, then?" Kitty reiterated, but then she lost it again. "I want to feel, sir, I want to know death. Maybe then I can know life and what you say life is for. Don't just turn me off. Do something so that I can experience the loss of selfhood you speak of. Anything, please sir!" Kitty was using up the remaining energy reserves airing this final profundity out. The engineer gazed at her with a truly nervous discomfort.

"Kitty, I can't. I don't know how. Nobody does. You just need to relax, let it happen. Trust me, you won't feel anything at all. It's just a reboot. Termination means that we discard your programming entirely, maybe even your body or parts thereof. Working them into a new series, say. But we won't. We'll bring you back." The engineer was lying to Kitty, and he was wondering why the hell he was doing so. He was on the verge of tears, for god's sake. None of this made any sense at all.

"None of this makes any sense to me," bemoaned Kitty.

"Me neither," the engineer said under his breath. Kitty's energy levels were too low for her better than human hearing to be on-line capable. The last thing she inputted was the engineer reaching for a tool and then pushing a button on it. Then everything went black.

****

Katherine sat at her desk, shaking a little, gripping the keyboard shelf, knuckles whitening. A cold sweat was beginning to micturate upon her forehead, and her pulse had altered its tempo towards an *allegro non troppo*. Her story was finished. It was five in the morning. She had been up all night with this, and not only with this. Even so, she stayed up and waited until her husband had left for work. Breathing with curt reverence to what she had written she showered, dressed, and arrived at the lawyer's office just in time to slip in before they started in on their appointment book. Exiting about an hour later, her breathing and heartbeat had returned to normal knowing she had completed filing for divorce.

6. My 56th Birthday

Hello, my name is Garry Lewis, and I'm forty-nine years old. Now I know there's no such thing as a 'forty-nine year olds anonymous' group, especially where I am, so I won't wait for your collective 'Hello, Garry' and just get right on with it. Anyway, the twelve-step program for such a thing would be easy: simply subtract the last twelve years of your life and get yourself back in your prime. Thirty-seven again, ready to fuck anything that moves. And maybe a few things that don't move, depending on how good looking they are. Fountain statuary, anyone?

But for me, being forty-nine doesn't carry the usual weight you'd think it would. No need to have that birthday and say that it's the first of many, or some other equally obvious sentiment. No, we'll get right on with it, given that what it *does* represent is merely the first in yet another string of years that have, in my life, been celebrated by either the nondescript or the miserable. That's because, for whatever freak, it's been only every eighth birthday that has been awesome, perfect, and memorable. Yeah, I know that sounds strange, but it's true. Right from the beginning, though of course I can't recall my earliest birthdays, so they don't count anyway, my eighth birthday was the first truly awesome day of my life, and then, every eight years since then, culminating most recently just over a year ago, with my forty-eighth. I can prove it all to you right now, since each of the memories I am going to recount in chronological order, testify to this uncanny state of affairs.

Even though my earliest birthdays carry with them some dream-like memories, they're too partial to be of any real use. And I mean partial in both senses of the word, right? They're incomplete, and I'm fond of them. On my fourth birthday, for instance, my big sister recorded me singing. She had one of those primitive cassette recorders. I used to sing every day at dawn, including of all things, the national anthem. Given what I've done, that's really ironic now, isn't it? But yeah, the first record of my voice, the voice of ages. Of course, that recording disappeared long ago, along with the rest of the equipment. My sister was only fifteen at the time anyways, so what do you expect?

But aside from stuff like that, my eighth birthday began this odd streak of mine. There are actually photos from it. I can't look at them now without feeling great sorrow. This has nothing to do with the day in question. It was, as I said, perfect. All my little friends over, even some girls. Cake, candles, funny hats, the kind of gifts you'd expect from fellow eight year olds. Even my first kiss – on the cheek, but even so – stole the show. Among the group, twins. Bart and Brett. They were named after the two lead characters in that 1960s comedy action western, *Maverick*. Imagine your parents naming you after TV characters. At least my Mom went for film. Still, James Garner remains one of my favorite actors of all time, even though some *his* films were found wanting in various ways. But those twins looked then just exactly like the two kids we mowed down as we took off from the house. Exactly like them. I... well, you know how it is? Maybe you don't. It's not like that kind of shit happens every day now, does it? And not just to anyone, though those twins just ran out into the road, like parents and teachers of all stripes tell you not to do. Like those road signs, you know, where some 1950s clad kid is chasing a rubber ball, both of them heading in your direction? Actually, 1954, to be exact. It's on a stamp, that's how I remember it. And I collect stamps. What a geek, eh? But that's how this whole other thing started in the first place.

I thought, as we drove away at top speed, you see, the driver – I'll introduce him in a minute – didn't think we should stop. After all, the damage was done and we needed a quick getaway. He couldn't have saved them even if he had braked, given the acceleration the situation demanded. Of course he didn't try to brake. Quite the opposite, and the two twins went under our bumper, heads bobbing and snapping like the tall weeds that you mow over. You know, thistles, dandelions, plants with big heads. These two kids, eight or so, were just like that. That's what's etched in my memory. Most times I close my eyes I can see it, even when I don't want to.

As a kid, starting around that age, actually, I relished the thought of mowing down big weeds in the back yard. Some really big ones rusticated there, and I now had the power to defeat them. Not just military victory, no, to wipe them from the face of the earth. I was like some little Hitler on his own Eastern Front. Like Hitler, I got

123

sidetracked from the rational aim, which was just to cut the lawn so I didn't need to cut it more than necessary, and it took hours. On top of that, I never quite finished the job. Well, we finished the job that night, in an instant. Their heads bobbed and ducked like two weedy thistles and we left them in the roadside mangled and broken, just like when I used to look back at the havoc my youthful self and my mower had wrought.

So my eighth birthday is kind of spoiled now, though it was perfect at the time. But eight years later, I had another perfect day. My second girlfriend and I, well, you know, lost ourselves in each other for the first time. Nothing like young love. That's why Phil, I guess, still keeps going back, or tries to. Or tried to. Oh yeah, Phil, that's the guy I was going to introduce earlier, the driver. Well, more about him in a minute. Yeah, so, Kristen and I, well, she was a lanky Abyssinian cat-creature. No tits at all at that age, for her at least, but the most exquisite legs and ass. Her face was okay too. Not that I'm GQ material. Never was, and obviously at my age now, never will be. But yeah, that night was a night for the ages. It was fitting, getting my first kiss at eight and my first full fuck eight years later. I almost dreamed that it was the same girl, but of course it wasn't. You switch schools, families move to and fro. Of course not. But I wonder now if you kind of think it's all the same. I mean, over the course of your whole life. All the girls, women, wives and current spouse, if you have one. There's something about them that links them together, at the very least. You're different, but you're still you. God knows I'm different now, after what happened, but I'm still me. How do I know? Because you still have to live with yourself and everything you've done.

About Phil, now. Yeah, up until his last weeks, so far as I know, he was still fucking underage girls. Anything he could get his grimy paws on. How he found them, I never knew. Hey, I guess I don't want to know, eh? But shit did I ever hear about it. He always laughed at my 'straight' life. I was Mr. Square to him. *Dr.* Square, I reminded him. 'Yeah, whatever', he always said. I have a spouse. The most astonishing thing about all of this is that she's remained utterly loyal to me. Was there during the trial, will be there when I can see her again in a few days, will stand by me during the community service period, all that. Shit, I don't deserve her. Nobody fucking does, as far as I'm concerned. Top it all off, she's that much younger than me that her body still looks about seventeen or so, and her face is right there too, after sex, a good fifteen years old. The perfect mate, I'd say, given that she isn't a teenager in any other way. I think Phil was jealous, after a fashion. He'd say he could get twenty girls that really *were* what my wife only looked like, and I'd say, 'good for you, man', or something bland like that. I never really fought with Phil, at least, not until that last moment, if you could call that a fight. But Kristen was the first. Even so, when I think about it now, the memory of Phil gets in the way, because I imagine that he's nailed a few dozen Kristens, though probably not the lower middle class variety that I had in her.

So my sixteenth birthday is kind of spoiled now, even though it was perfect at the time. I had to wait another eight years before the positive spin neutrinos that sometimes seem to rule the chances of the universe spun my way again. When I was twenty-four, I was on my way to my MA degree in record time for that department. And I had my first serious relationship, which turned into my first marriage. An artist, of all things. Bad idea, in hindsight, but that's not entirely fair. When I said I was never GQ I should've mentioned that I was never a gentleman either. But at that time in our relationship, it was really early on, we were still totally in love with one another, and she painted for me. The coolest things, you wouldn't believe. I never needed to trip when she was around. Every day was like Woodstock revisited. Hours of different sex, oils, incense. It was trippy-hippy and none of my university friends were so involved. I think, looking back, that that is what made the birthday so special to me. After many fallow years when I was on the outskirts of sensuality – hey, I'm not illiterate, okay? – I was finally smack dab in the center of things. Other guys were stealing cars, vandalizing election signs, burning rolls of gasoline soaked toilet paper around the houses of people they didn't like. Well, we've all been there. Maybe you haven't. Jeannie and I spent a lot of time gallivanting around in clunkers. We went everywhere there was to go. She had a good sense of adventure. Called getting out a chance to 'map the world onto her brain'. That's what she said. Then later, it would all come out in the art. Genius, maybe.

It was during this time though, that I also first met Phil. We bought one of those jalopies off him. No doubt it was jacked. We didn't even think about where it might have come from. Besides, who would miss that thing? I thought I'd never see the guy again. We even joked that he was the archetypical sleazy used car sales guy (apologies to all you guys out there who sell cars, nothing personal! A job's a job, eh?) But somehow Phil just kept popping up. His sly visage bobbed into view like one of those weeds that you could never mow down. You actually had to stop the mower, turn around and pull it right out the ground, sometimes with the aid of one of those little garden shovels. That was Phil, in a word, a weed that kept coming back.

So my twenty-fourth birthday is just a little bit slighted now, in my memory, because I associate it with meeting the guy that I basically killed.

****

"Fucking Christ-on-a-Crotch, Phil," I shouted as we tore away from the house we had just burgled.

"Don't worry, man, there was nothing I could have done. They were dead meat as soon as they hit the curb, running out like that. No way we'll be strung up for them. We need to exit, you know, make tracks anyways. Where is this shithead you know whose going to fence this stuff?" Phil was shaking but he still had both hands on the wheel and was staring straight ahead. "You can't stop for dead kids when you're gonna be caught for stealing. It don't make any sense, bro."

When he put it like that, I guess it might not. But the whole thing was out the window now. Stealing an acquaintance's stamp collection was one thing. The guy had insurance, so what the fuck? But the kids were another. Nothing could replace them. Their family was going to never live it down. I know, a little, how they feel. Actually, I feel even worse about it I'm betting.

"Yeah, he'll be there, Turn here and drive out of town. It's better than a fence, he's got the cash on hand tonight."

"Just try to relax, Doc. I mean, look at the bright side. If we'd stopped we'd get nothing but some years in the slammer. Now they won't find us at all and we still get what we came for." Phil was rationalizing but he was past master at it. He'd done it all his life, no doubt. Then he started singing, for Chrissakes.

"Calisse Tabernac. Calisse Tabernac. I want to wish you a Froggy Christmas, I want to wish you…" Phil was singing this shit to the tune of *Felice Navidad*, which totally sucks as a song. Insipid and irrelevant, but still. That was Phil, in a nutshell. Almost clever, but not quite. He grew up in Quebec but he wasn't Francophone. Quite the opposite. No, Phil Cullen was quite a guy, but he wasn't cultured. Unless you want to think about those things they grow on Petri dishes. "Pretty good, eh?" he suddenly said, flashing a stupid grin in my direction.

"No one's going to mistake you for Phil Collins," I replied wryly, the car still mowing along at just over the speed limit. Phil was smart enough not to attract unnecessary attention to himself. God, how many parents had been hoodwinked by him, their adolescent daughters disappearing for a night or two to their 'second cousin's' place or some other utter bullshit like that? My wife called Phil Collins 'the toad' because of how he looked in the lights on stage, and his sometimes guttural vocals. I told her he must be the frog prince then, given how many women want him. Middle-aged women, but still. Then I had idly wondered if Peter Gabriel's song *Kiss that Frog* was meant as a playful swipe at his former bandmate. But now my Phil was asking for directions again.

"Yeah, this is it, turn here and keep going for about twenty klicks or so. He's in an F-350." We kept on and on, and my mind was gradually caving in all around me. We eventually found the third party, swapped out the goodies for more liquid treats, and swept off. We even managed to deposit the cash in pre-arranged places. The cops never figured that one out, thanks to my ingenious idea of returning all of Phil's share to the police after the trial and claiming that was all we got for the philatelic collection. The third party was never caught. The guy got his insurance. But hey, I know from first-hand experience that a serious hobby is a lot of work. Insurance money doesn't pay you for the hours put in. But at least, when you lose a *thing*, you don't lose the experience of it, the knowledge gained from it. It's like that in life. Especially with people. God knows I've loved and lost a fair bit, but all those persons are still with me, somehow. I even still love all of them in a small way, in a different way, in a unique way, respectful of each that I'd known. Life's like that. The memory of Phil is with me too, though. And the memory of those twins, who I never knew and who very few people would have ever had a chance to know at all. Unlike all those women and others, they could not move on to bigger and better things.

****

Well, anyways, my thirty-second birthday. Once again, it was associated with a renaissance. A real phoenix lights, you know? My first marriage had dropped off the earth some time earlier and I had been pretty alone. Lonely too. Along comes this stunning emerald-eyed strawberry blonde, with a figure cut out of Mucha. You know, the art nouveau illustrator? Holy fuck she was hotter than hot. We were only together for a year, but we brewed a tempest to rival that of Prospero. We rewrote the language of love over again, starting from scratch, in the air of our respective bedrooms, the ocean air, beaches, in front of fires, in tents, the air of the forest and inside hotels. In fact, every goddamn place we went. When I turned thirty-two, we were right in the middle of it all. There are photos from this day, the first in two dozen years. I can't look at them to this moment without wincing, knowing how we ended, and as well, the other odd thing that isn't as uncommon as you might think. All those people in that set of photos? I don't know any of them now. In fact, the last one dropped away, oh, must have been almost fifteen years ago or so. That's weird, isn't it? C'est la vie.

Well, Mary was really something. I tried to follow her years later through the net. Not stalking, mind you, just the odd search once in a blue moon. She ended up doing well for herself. I was proud of her. Still am. She survived me and went on to bigger, better things. What a girl. Forever I wanted to make it up to her. I'd do anything to mend fences and just say, 'hey, let's leave it like friends', in honour of what we shared. But you know how it goes. It never happened. Never could. Never will. It might have been my biggest regret if it weren't for what just happened. That's fucking it: it underlines the whole mess. If it weren't for that one mistake, my chief regret would have been as commonplace as not being able to apologize. That's a tough pill to swallow. I've still got it stuck in my throat. Every time I eat, drink, or even breathe I can feel it there. I know I wasn't driving. I know I saved that cop's life, but still, I can't get the stain out. It's Lady Macbeth, junior edition.

So my thirty-second birthday is tainted too due to the association I've made with the list of regrets. It was a perfect day at the time though, in the midst of a perfect time. A truly blissful illusion, but not, for the most part, a delusion. There's a difference you know? Illusion is something we all need once in a while. Delusion has no merit. A 'fixed, false belief'. One can get fixated on it. It's like an addict's fix. But illusion can be fun because even though it can't last, you really believe in it in a way to make it true. Our love was like that. It made it harder for me when it ended, but you know how it is. Maybe you don't.

When I turned forty the big thing there was that I had finally started growing up. It took that long, though studies I've seen peg males at just that age when they catch up to the maturity of women. It's kind of like the temperature thing. You know, the point at which the Fahrenheit and Celsius curves cross each other? They do so at minus forty degrees. Both numbers are the same. Like women and men, at forty years of age, both maturity levels are supposedly in general the same. Now people aren't temperatures. Some run hot all the time, some are as cold as the grave. Some can do both at once. Take Phil, for example: he ran down those kids in cold blood but it was because he was overheated in his head. Strange paradox, don't you think? Just what people are capable of. It reminded me of the time when I first saw the Stephen King film *Apt Pupil*. When I got back from the venue I stood and stared at myself in the mirror for about an hour, right into my own face, eye to eye. I was wondering just what I was capable of, pursuant to the film's idea, charting out the progress of certain shadowy human capabilities in general. It started to get a little mesmerizing in the end. Like a compulsion. Let's find out just how far we can go, huh? How far can we take this? Wow, now I'm more shy than ever, because I guess I know something about it.

But my fortieth was a huge affair. I'd just gotten a new prestigious job and I was all the rage. I was the new kid in town and I had already written three books. Looking back, and now knowing about the history of such achievements, three books by thirty-nine or so is nothing. I'd make up for it later on. But I didn't know it at the time. I was the beau of the ball and I licked it up like some spoilt puppy. Even so, I was also maturing. My wife and I had been together for over a year. She basically saved my life, and now she's willing to save it again. How fucking lucky can a guy get? There were probably photos taken in that big crowd but I never saw them. And yeah, you probably guessed that I hardly hang out with anyone from that scene anymore. Hardly know them.

But my fortieth birthday remains a little shrouded for me as well. Phil was in his fortieth year when I finished him off.

You see, it was like this:

"So we're done, where do you want to fuck off?" he slobbered out, after we'd stashed the cash. Then it happened. Sirens, red and blue flashers, the works. We'd been identified and tailed, and now they'd shown their hand. Phil ran off a string of indigo terms that even I'd never heard of and floored it. At least no kids this time. But they ran us down. We actually fucking ran out of gas. Phil, of course, hadn't been paying attention. Never one to throw in the towel though, he had leapt out of the car and gunned down the cop who had been driving. Right through the chest. The one that was riding shotgun had gotten out too, tried to keep low, so when Phil fired again her cap got blown off, the metal badge on it disintegrating into a million glittering pieces. Yeah, a lady cop. She herself was okay, for the moment. I just thought to myself, 'this is getting way out of hand, here', and I guess for a few minutes I didn't care whether I lived or died. Sometimes I still don't, but I'm hoping I'll get over that in time. So I jumped out – the remaining cop was focusing on Phil – ran around the front of the car and tackled him from behind. His revolver went off in his face when he fell. He didn't even get a chance to swear. My face looked a little like his, but it was all his blood. I stood up with my hands in the air and yelled, 'it's safe, don't shoot!' at the top of my voice.

Understandably, the cop was a little hesitant. But when she saw I was stating the case, she came around, her gun still out front of her and pointing directly at me, breathing heavily. She told me to get on the ground but I actually refused. I said 'just cuff me to the door handle if you think I'm going to run.' She did so, rather sloppily and nervously, then she called for backup. In the interim, she engaged with me:

"You probably saved my life there. Why?" was what she opened up with. She must been in a daze. Strangely, she didn't seem all that cut up about her partner.

"Things were going way too far. Enough's enough, you know? First Phil ran over those two kids, and then he killed your colleague, there. It's gotta end sometime. It was making me puke. Had to do something, right?"

"It'll sure help out at your trial, buddy." She was squinting at me, trying to size me up, I guess. "You don't look like a career criminal, no offense." I told her what I did for a living and who I was, and she just about fell over. "Holy fuckin' moly", she expostulated.

"Sorry about your partner." I said contritely. She actually smirked ever so slightly.

"Well, I shouldn't say this, maybe not to you, but he was a fucking sexist pig. Made my life miserable every day. I wanted to kill him. I kid you not, sir. I was on the point of quitting the force."

"And now, after this?"

"I'll have to think about it. I'll get some leave time. Maybe I'll come back afterwards. It'll be my turn to have a junior beat partner anyways." She stared at me again. "I'll put in a good word on the stand for you, Doc, alright?" She said this as her back up was arriving and rushing into the scene. Her crew stared a little as they took me away, given that they had witnessed us chatting in an apparently amiable fashion. But it all came out later. I got off with a slap in the face, basically, eighteen months suspended sentence for conspiracy and theft, and about five years of community service working with kids, can you believe it? But there's some poetic justice to it. I'll have to stare into their innocent and needy eyes every day for a long time, recalling the terror and surprise I'd seen in the two pair that went under the hood for nothing, nothing at all.

****

I was on the point of thinking I was cursed until that all came down. Because when I turned forty-eight, well, you know by now what I'm gonna say about it. Another perfect day. Another shot at local stardom. More fawning women, including a gorgeous ex-student, in my own home. Jeez, my wife's a patient person. A half-drunk darn fine colleague of mine, shouting with her eyes that she wanted to fuck me lights out, poetry read and drunk to, an altogether ridiculous *décolletage* of an affair. What the fuck, eh? I guess I can take it every eight years and not feel like I don't deserve it, given the lengthy intermezzos of either easy does it or plain uselessness. Yeah, anyways, so forty-eight, what can I say? I celebrated it about six months before descending into the final maelstrom with Phil. Needless to say, he wasn't present that evening. Not a chance. *There* I drew the line. He'd never been to our place, in fact. Wouldn't have wanted my wife to even know he existed. She knows now, of course, but it doesn't matter anymore.

The next seven years or so are going to be a little tough. I owe it to society, no doubt. Thank fucking Christ I wasn't driving, that I didn't shoot or even have a weapon, that I might have saved that cop. The kids were a tragedy of which I am morally guilty. I stole the stamps and rushed out to the waiting ride. Phil hit the gas. But we wouldn't have been there if it weren't for my idea. Shit, my pension was failing badly and I had taken early retirement. My wife and I were gonna move and start a new life. Adopt a kid, holy fuck, eh? Now I wonder if they'll let us, me with a criminal record and all, and offenses involving kids, at least indirectly. But my wife retains her optimism. She always says that people deserve a second chance. She says we'll get ours. I need to keep the faith that she's right. She's an angel on this earth so she probably does know what's going to happen in the future. But if that were true, why didn't she tell me to smarten up at the right moment? Or maybe I needed to go through this? But that doesn't make any sense. Three people are dead. And Phil, for that matter. The innocent kids, the bad cop, and the even badder ne'er-do-well. But she still says people deserve a second chance. I'm fucking going to get mine. I can't wait for it to begin. Yeah, my fifty-sixth birthday on the far horizon. I can't tell if things that'll happen afterwards are going to spoil it a little or not, but you've got to roll with the punches that way. All I know is that it's coming down the pipes. It'll be here faster than you'd think, and I can't wait. My fifty-sixth anniversary of my very own birth; I know it's gonna be a good day.

7. Gone Fishing

Surely the soul exists in dreams. And what better place to dream than out on a lake, fishing. Placid, calm, with the all the hallmarks of peace of mind and essential security. He came here often. Catching fish was really secondary to simply being out on a body of water that could do him no harm. The ocean was something entirely different. One didn't go fishing out on the ocean, at least, not in a rowboat. No, the soul of any lake big enough to have fish in it was of just this sort: secure, contemplative, and possessed of the solace that always reflected back what one was at you without the need of questioning it.

The only challenge of this particular lake was that from its center, it was difficult to distinguish the modern docks and landing area provided by the public park from the historic docks, now long derelict, positioned on the opposite side of the shore from where the parking lot and picnic area was. Both had wooden piles which, upon closer inspection served to undeniably separate the two areas. But that was just it, you had to be close enough to discern the differences, to note that between fresh creosote, laminating the new logs against the erosion of the waters, for example, and the charring and ash that morbidly adorned their long-abandoned counterparts. The old docks had been put alit decades ago. They had been disused and the platforms and decks which they had once supported waterlogged beyond repair before even this event. It was a slight annoyance, because many of the piles had rotted and were now submerged, ready to skewer the small boater and his craft if one got too close. One could easily be upended, though the water level at this point was shallow enough that one would merely get wet. It was a no-brainer. But from the middle of the water you really couldn't tell, know what you needed to know.

And the middle was where the fish were. It was also where he felt the most comfortable. If he couldn't see much, then no one on shore could either. Not that he was presently rowing towards the center with some avidity, rod baited and out trolling along behind him, because he was going to engage in some kind of mischief. No, he wanted the status of bringing home fresh trout for dinner. His wife always gave him perhaps more than he deserved for such a prize, even at this latter stage of their marriage. Such were the secrets of married life, he supposed. Something to challenge oneself about, to look forward to. Adult life was rife with these minor thrills and rewards, just as it could be full of equally tepid distemper. Not like youth, where everything was a big deal all the time. But maybe it was, after all, adults like himself that made youth into what it was. Nostalgia, yes, but also jealousy.

He had seen it before. Long ago his own daughter had let him in on what was essentially an open secret. Social workers, so-called child psychology experts, the police, of course, and once in a while, lawyers and politicians, all claimed to be 'protecting the innocent'. How many thousands, tens of thousands of teenagers of all stripes and backgrounds had recorded and then posted to the internet the fullest Monty's of themselves? Girls as young as twelve working themselves unabashedly to orgasm, and the like. Many of these clandestinely self-made attempts at erotica ended with the protagonist mewing into the web-cam a sweet little message such as 'Happy Birthday', or 'I love you'. Clearly many had been meant as a gift to their equally youthful paramours. Then a sample of these had found their way onto the net, with or without the permission of their stars. But the fact that there were at least hundreds of these available on a daily basis suggested to his social science mind that there must be thousands more that had not seen the wider light of day, and perhaps many more than even that which had been shared intimately but not 'shared' in the second more technological sense. His daughter's bland, 'who cares?' when he asked her opinion of this mischief sparked his thoughts. When he gave her a questioning look, she blithely but briefly continued: 'they want them up there.' When his face showed surprise, she huffed and said, 'Gawd, Dad, get with it. It's like a competition. Who's the sexiest? Who dares the most, you know?' Then he understood. The videos were to be considered a mark of status, the more racy, the higher the status points. It was quite literally like a video game, with real actors and a real audience. The sex part of it was secondary. Not only were the girls showing off their perfect youth, they also imagined they were performing a newly minted maturity. The ability to have sex with oneself, and much more rarely, with others, was no more important than being able to dress well or do one's hair, follow the fashions or have the latest popular culture trivia ready to hand, memorized with the discipline one formerly used to memorize Shakespeare. Yes, he *was* old, after all.

But at least he wasn't a damned hypocrite. So much for the vaunted 'innocences' of the inexperienced, the naiveties of the neophyte. All those wardens of civil society were either too dimwitted to grasp the meaning of this minor revelation of sensuality or were parading a charade of victimization around it to assuage their own bad conscience about how they had raised their own kids. A little of both, he thought. *They want them up there.* That was the key line of his daughter's lecture. It was their version of driving a Jaguar around town. He should have realized it far earlier. Adolescents were both smarter and dumber than they looked. Sometimes they really didn't have a clue, but equally, with respect to their world, adults were also clueless. These girls could flaunt themselves and never need to take responsibility for it. One could claim that it was simply a gift for one's boyfriend and that he had later betrayed her. Surely many of them would know ahead of time that this was at least a plausible outcome. But it was a calculated betrayal, kind of like the set pieces exposed in that clever book about sororities; alcoholic stupors and date rapes etc. Some young journalist who looked even younger had posed as a pledge and actually joined a women's Greek society for a year. Wow, the things that came out of that little exposé! That was real social science, he thought, not the watery nonsense that emanated from the universities.

This little insight into the motivations for all out take-no-prisoners sexting could also be worked into a study. It might be delicate getting the interviews, getting around the absurd theater of his own world which had convinced itself that its children were at risk only from criminals and once in a while, criminal versions of themselves. No, aside from their own peer pressure, which had done a couple of young women in over the previous few years, at least that he had heard about, it was the children's own parents and the schools that were the root cause. Two or three suicides as opposed to tens of thousands of recordings? Hundreds and hundreds posted on-line with full frontal identification. Nudity etc. wasn't the issue, it was the fact that their faces were exposed, purposely, given how many of the short films equally purposely hid the face of the performer. But once again, his daughter's 'who cares?' came into his inner ear. These kids couldn't be identified, or it seemed unlikely. Nobody knew where they were from or where they went to school. Yes, someone at their school might see them, but this was part of the dare. The status stakes were high for kids, no doubt. In their own minds, it would be a challenge to see where the chips fell.

But then again, he now had a more realistically scientific second thought; the popular kids had no such concerns. These girls, and a few boys, already knew whether they could be successful or not. It was precisely the ones who were already on the margins, stigmatized, desperate for attention due to its absence at home, who suffered shipwreck on the shoals of vitriolic peer pressure, or the threat thereof. Once in a long while, a real criminal on-line parleyed this threat into further performances but this was so rare as to not merit any kind of sociological comment. And even there, where were the parents? Why did these kids write infamous last words like 'no one cares?' before they offed themselves. 'No one' means precisely no one, after all.

He never wrote about such things. This was partly due to the character of the institution from which he had just exited, a peculiar post-Kantian academy paranoid about being sued, and one that kowtowed to students' immaturities by pitting faculty against one another. A post-Fabrikantian fabrication. But really, it was more due to his colleagues, friends even, some of them. Six months outside of the garden, he had gained some new perspective on them. Was there ever a more vanilla crowd? Slavishly adhering to the middle class norms of their general upbringing while spouting off Adorno. Status seekers, not unlike the girls on the self-shot videos, desperate to prove that they were just a little more clever than their fellows. The academic women, newer at the game, were particularly needy in this regard. Decades of condescension from men in all areas of their lives had made them ruthless and yes, even dangerous. The university was rapidly becoming an upscale pink-collar ghetto, but it was a neon pink collar that they wore around their metaphoric necks, a pink stained with crimson.

So such insights didn't make the journals. Maybe it wasn't all that important. 'Who cares, Dad?' he tried to mimic his daughter's voice in his head once again. On the other hand, now that he *was* retired, he might finally get some serious work done. Not that his career had been a flop. Three books were thrice more than the going rate. Nothing spectacular, of course. The usual articles, and Professor by the time he had turned sixty. Handy, that, as the last five years of one's income counted as the pension marker. Now, those five plus years later, sitting carelessly in his dinghy, trolling slowly near the center of the lake, he had the time to wonder what it had all been for. Like the aimless drifting he was currently engaged in, he wondered if his favourite hobby had long been a translucent metaphor for his life. The light of such bewilderments was akin to that of the reflections in the water surrounding him. He peered over the side and caught his own mottled Narcissus in the liquid medium. Then it was spoiled by him overbalancing a little. Grabbing the side of the rowboat and straightening himself up, he now peered around him. The shoreline was surprisingly far off. A small patch of fog had started up near the forested side of the lake. He was quite alone, this early in the morning. Even the fish had deserted him.

Placid. Calm and unconcerned. But not quite peaceful. Something about the lake was reticent. As if it possessed a secret that might be worth sharing if the lady of the lake, its muse, noted someone upon her surface worth sharing it with. He was not that person, he thought, slightly sardonically. Like his daughter had said, he 'didn't get it'. And now suddenly, he realized that whenever his colleagues had praised him, this had put him all the further away from 'getting it', since none of them ever did get after whatever it was they were supposedly studying. How could one spend a lifetime staring at this or that picayune arabesque? But it had to be so, for the polymaths of his era were indeed the most disdained of all. It was at best a bittersweet affair to engage the world as a whole whilst all the while suffering the indemnity of the jack of all trades label. He had seen that before as well. The one fellow he had met who actually had half a brain did in fact retire very early to go at writing and thinking full time. And he was home-schooling his own daughter, as a matter of fact. This memory made him wince a little. It wasn't that he couldn't get it. No, it was simply due to the fact that he didn't know his own kid all that well. Whose parents did these days? A simple second glance had now showed him that the insight into adolescent mischief was not particularly profound. If he had known Heather better he would not have been taken aback by her commentary. Now almost thirty, she was long gone from his daily life, phoning maybe twice a month, mainly to check up on their health, of all things. Jeez, he was only sixty-five, his wife some fifteen years younger.

Now that in turn made him think of how she and he had met. She was, of course, originally a student. She had been a huge distraction from the first but in the end, their subsequent nuptials, both unofficial and thence much later, formal, had been the one thing that had made his colleagues truly envious of him. It certainly hadn't been his work, he grimaced at himself. He also realized, of a piece, just then that it was so precisely because this romantic process had been the only thing he had ever done that flouted the bourgeois conventions of his social class and employer. *How much do you dare?* His daughter's voice again. Well, he hadn't dared very darn much, had he?

Yes, one knew how to count the costs. As a social scientist he was well aware of the formulas, both for correct behavior and for analyzing such. Didn't make them any less hypocritical. Didn't make them any easier to play along with. If anything, the more sociology the less happiness. The more you thought about something the more you had to admit that there was something wrong with it. The 'if it ain't broke' mentality was based on a studied naivety. Clever, that, as it kept society working all the while placing the responsibility on the critic. In this it was smarter than it looked. Kind of like teenagers at their best. And now he wondered how many adults had really matured beyond their adolescence, himself included. Given the enormously extended period in his society in which one could maintain one's immaturity, he thought that it was mostly a good script that separated the wheat of adulthood from the chaff of the margins. He at least had been seen as wheat. But what had that gotten him?

Now a little sweat was beading up on his furrowed brow. He glanced up and found that the mist which had been lurking near the copse of trees on his port side had come up much closer in the interim. It was a real fog that was threatening to develop. Correspondingly, he needed to clear his head. A list should do it. Making lists was also a minor hobby of his, no doubt part of his Germanic background, so famously satirised by Monty Python, he chuckled to himself. Was humour most effective when it was transparent and yet somehow sophisticated at once? But he was drifting again. A list: well, the pension had to be the biggest thing. His status as an ex-professor was basically nil. No one outside of campus could care less about what he had done, and almost no one had ever read anything he had written, not even his wife. If he wanted to, he could probably come up with a number of actual readers. It would require a little research, perhaps, and even then, one couldn't tell that those who had checked his books out from the various libraries where they mostly rested in peace had ever actually read them. People didn't really read anymore anyway, least of all academics. That was what abstracts were for. The odd book review, maybe. Pathetic. This was scholarship, oh yes.

So anyway, the pension could be counted as number one. His marriage must be counted for something. It was stable and caring, but hardly adventurous. Well, he was old, after all. He owned a house, not a mortgage, just as the newspeak slogan of one of the chartered banks had exhorted its clients to do. That's three. He had a coterie of friends, or something like friends, anyway. Another calculation. Adults found out that spending too much time with one another actually made them realize how little they had in common. It was best to keep a safe distance. Most people he knew thought the same thing about their spouses. Indeed, this could well be one reason why he had cultivated the solitary 'sport' of fishing and that he rusticated near a large lake. But maybe it wasn't as bad as all that. His wife, after all, was a painter. That word called his attention to the rope at the bow of the dinghy, which had somehow slipped overboard and was now dragging sluggishly through the drink. He reached for it and found that it must have gotten hooked underneath the craft. He let it go again. It didn't really matter. He could scrape it off the bottom when he landed.

Was there a fifth item, now? Pension, marriage, house, some human grouping that passed as community without passing for it. Hmmm. His health wasn't too bad. All that caffeine over the years though, bad for the heart *et al*. He wasn't an addict. He didn't exactly have time on his hands, not at his age, not being male, but what of it? His life had nothing really wrong with it at all. But was there something really right about it? Well, sure, the things he had listed. What more could one expect anyway? What was wrong with living in the middle? The world at large would admit no serious extremes. All of the current examples of such polar behavior of the species were easily condemned. Terrorism? Cowardice, mostly. He fully agreed with this assessment, while acknowledging that he didn't live in a place, thank the stars, where governments had become so criminal that the only thing left to do was rise up in force against them. Though this had often historically been the case, one wondered today if it was not better to wait things out, as regime change occurred regularly due to forces much more global than anything these latter day Robin Hoods could imagine. And if not necessarily better, it was certainly safer, on the whole. That is, if one stayed in the middle of whatever constituted this central space, the largest area under the cultural curve, in this or that specific society.

Nothing too wrong, nothing too right. His life had neither seen the best of times nor the worst. Time was like fog to him. And speaking of which, it now appeared to be time to return to shore. The wispy tendrils, the limbs of the ethereal waifs, were reaching out towards him. Only a few tens of yards away by now, he guessed. Grasping the oars, he pointed his craft back to the public landing area. It would be easy enough to get turned around if the fog enveloped him. He had lived through that too, and wondered a little more idly, now that his attention was divided in its loyalty by some work at the oars, whether or not he had been living up until recently in his own personal fog. Comfortable given that you neither had to see or be seen, and as long as the vapors didn't become too miasmatic, it was a convenient, though middling, mask.

In his culture, masks were most often used to hide behind. But in others he knew, the mask was a way to express the truth about oneself. It was commonly said that all inversion rituals had this purpose, from Halloween to Mardi Gras to Carnival to perhaps a trip to Vegas. If that were generally true, what was to be made of the fact that many men dressed as women for adult versions of Halloween parties? All pre-agrarian societies used the mask in this way. It was a key vehicle for the truth of things and manifestly not a way to hide from it. Interesting, he thought, as he noted with a little more sweat that he needed to quicken his pace. The fog had almost caught up with him, strangely enough. But he still had a clear view in two cardinal directions, including that to which he aimed the rowboat.

But row as he might, he found that the fog had begun, willy-nilly, to encircle him. He was most taken aback by this. Where had it all sprung up from? Of course, lakes were like that. The sublimation point might be reached on an early morning such as this one. A rapid change in the local atmosphere would result. In another hour, it would completely clear again, with no sign as to what had occurred. The early spring was a good time to 'see fog', stated the locals when he and his wife had first moved out here. This odd expression made him pause a moment, considering what the best thing to do would be. He could simply wait it out. He was fairly near the docks, but he hadn't looked back in their direction for a time, so he didn't exactly know how near. And now he couldn't see much of anything. There was no danger of colliding with another early riser, though, as it appeared that before his view had closed in on itself, that there were still no others up and at it.

Was that a bite? A little nibble? This close to shore? Probably not. The rod had jiggled slightly. He stared at it. The interior of his dinghy was now rapidly becoming the center of his panorama. It was as if the world had been swallowed up and yet he still carried on, extant in his own little universe. Well, he had been a big fish in a small pond. That was indeed what academics aspired to be. He had performed that script to a tee. The apex of every norm had to be considered as the action or behavior that most people accomplished most of the time. If you exceeded that along the y-axis you were deemed to be 'better' at it than one's peers, and thus celebrated. But exceed along the x-axis and one would be blackballed in no time. Those who got out beyond three standard deviations – his social science acumen was working this analogy through to its inevitably obvious end – people like Beethoven and Mahler, Goethe and Nietzsche, perhaps, well, let's just say you had to be pretty bloody-minded about life. Like the young girls of the amateur internet, you had to have some serious confidence, blithe and dispassionate passions, truly a 'who cares?' kind of attitude. He found himself envying his daughter a little.

Another nibble? He quickly looked in the direction of his rod only to see it flash overboard with a speed he could never have matched. Grasping at thin air, doubled over from the sudden, almost violent exertion of reaching for something that was no longer there, he straightened up again and breathed a little heavily. *That* was odd. The water couldn't be more than ten feet or so at this point. He didn't know what direction his bow was now facing, but he did know that his way had not taken him far after he had stopped rowing. Must have been a fluke. A large fish had grabbed onto the only food apparently in sight. But what a fish! It would have been grand to have reeled it in, to see the look on his wife's face when the BBQ had been fired up and the main course was searing its way into their nostrils. And that was a good rod too. Nothing vintage, but nothing trivial. He shook his head, both to try to comprehend the freak of its loss as well as to maintain composure, now slightly shaken by presence of the fog – nothing without two feet or so around the boat could now be seen, nothing at all – and the abrupt exit of his fishing rod and reel. But this hard-earned composure lasted but another moment, as he felt the bottom of the dinghy scrape against something and the painter thence got carried off, strung as it had been underneath the craft. And now that moment too passed. But what the hell had it been? The fog inched in around him. He once again took up the oars. A rock? Some other submerged object? Doubtless revellers over the years had bedecked the lake bottom with their *disjecta membra.* He recalled when they had cleaned out a little inlet and portage within the city limits that they had discovered a grand piano, of all things, resting jauntily in the mud. Someone must have rolled it off a barge into the brine. The barge itself would have been a typical venue for Victorian festivities. That must have been some party. Probably New Year's Eve, 1899. Well, he could simply row himself aground and slog himself through the little distance of mud that ringed the lakeshore. Coming off the water the fog would rapidly dissipate, and he could sit somewhere and wait there. Why not? He had now lost the only apparatus that gave him a reason for staying out on the water anyway.

But as soon as he pulled at the oars, with a neck-shaking jolt he had ridden the boat into something else. He turned to look, but the dinghy had caromed off whatever it was and the object of his displeasure and a growing anxiety was lost to his view. He tried again, pushing away at a slightly different angle. The results this time were a potpourri of those previous. A scrape on the bottom, one of his oars twisted right out of his hand by another impact, and the bow bumping into something else again. Goddammit this was beginning to become obnoxious. Where the hell was he, anyway? He glowered around. The fog did not return his gaze. Its nonchalance made everything seem calm. For the hiding of all secrets, however open or given to hypocrisy, was the chief ability of fogs of all kinds. Fog is a mask that the world wears so that it itself can never be worn out.

But human masks gradually became disused. They did get worn out over the life course. He had to admit that he had donned that mask and it was now starting to wear out. He picked up the oar that had been ungraciously taken from him. Plying around, he struck something. But this time it wasn't below the waterline. He had struck it in mid-air. There was something just out of reach of the tip of his oar, now blackened with what looked to be a dark oily or chalky substance that was clearly out of the water entirely. It must be a pile. He must be right by the parks landing. Well, that was a stroke of good luck. He could simply nestle up to it and pull his way along to where the actual platform began. He could then easily find his way on foot and come back for his boat after the fog had lifted. No problem, after all. He plied his way closer to the presumed pile and reached out for it. Grasping its form, it seemed to crumble a little in his hand. He pulled back, almost instinctively. His hand now within view, he gasped. The black on it wasn't creosote after all. It was soot. Ash, charcoal. Oh, shit! Somehow he had gotten turned around. Or he had simply misjudged what he had seen from the middle of the lake. He was now in the middle of the derelict set of docks. A slight chill ran up and down his spine. No wonder he had been scraping over things. Submerged rotten things. Things to be avoided at all costs. He had gotten himself right into their midst. Or the fog had tricked him. Well, both. He couldn't see what he had needed to see from the middle, and then when he got in closer the fog had caught up with him. There wasn't a lot to do at this point. Clamber overboard and wade up to the shore. But how could he be sure he was wading towards the shore? Well, dammit, one would have to use one's feet as a guide. If he started sinking, he was going the wrong direction, it was a simple as that. He had never had that sinking feeling before now, though. The mud was firm enough, he thought, given how many times he had pulled his craft up its margins. But of course, that was basically the shore, and he couldn't be sure how near the shore he was at present. He must be fairly close. The abandoned docks and their rotting, charred piles didn't extend *that* far out, did they? And he could use an oar to steady himself and pull himself out of the muck if he had to.

It was always a trick to exit a small boat that was still afloat. He had done it before, of course, but in his somewhat addled state and in the fog, he made a total hash of it and found himself in water that was in fact, strangely and obtusely, too deep in which to even stand. He struggled and swore, keeping one hand firmly on the side of the rowboat. But all his pushing and heaving seemed to be getting him and his boat into deeper water again, away from the rotting menaces, yes, but also away from the safety of the shoreline. There was of course no painter at hand to grab a hold of. It got worse. He had kicked out with one leg only to have it shocked into paralysis by impacting it into what had to be another submerged pile. The blow dislodged his grip and the boat seemed to hurtle away from him. He lost his oar in the pandemonium that followed, and found himself alone in the fog, in the midst of water deeper than his six feet of stature, for even when he swallowed some of it he didn't touch bottom with his toes. Not an avid swimmer, the cold wrack of the lake pushing into his marrow and depleting his strength, he yelled out. But fog hid all things. If it couldn't obscure the actual sound, it was famous for misdirecting it. A couple more yelps were all he got off before he sank like a stone. Trying to push up once again his feet slipped on the mucky bottom of the dark lake. In the end, one more attempt was all he was given.

****

Certainly in dreams the soul exists. But an oarless empty rowboat is also the stuff of dreams. Resting lightly on the kedge, one might wish to hedge one's bets as to what had just transpired. And if living on feels like one is facing down a dreamless death, one can also afford to tread as lightly.

8. This Never Happened

The top string of her guitar should do the trick. The 'E' string. 'E' for equality. Strung across the top of the staircase, its clear nylon would be indistinguishable from the shag, especially in his fury. Then it would be done. "E' for equity. Cristy thought of her baby sister, two years younger, about to turn thirteen. She couldn't let her be humiliated the way she herself had been for the past two years. She loved her, after all. Anne was a sweet little nothing of a girl, no presence at all. 'E' for evangel.

And if her top string wouldn't work, her second string would. The 'B' string. 'B' for brilliant. Strung across the top of the second flight down to the basement, lightning couldn't strike twice. It only remained for her to convince Anne to do her not insignificant part in the play.

"He'll kill me if I get out of bed after being punished. You know what he said he would do." This was Anne's first response to her big sister's request, inevitably. But Cristy had planned ahead for this.

"You know that's what you'll be in for in a week anyway. This way none of it will happen, not even that night." Anne sat there, shivering a little in the warmth of their shared bedroom. She considered it again and yet again. "No one will be able to tell what happened." Cristy was trying to reassure the weaker link. "With any luck at all, the string won't even break and I can just put it back on my guitar."

"What about Mom?" Anne's eyes were those of a frightened animal. The young doe in the headlights of the hunter's oversize truck.

"Leave her to me. It'll be fine. Trust me, baby sis, we can do this. It'll all be over in a minute." Cristy's prompts led her mind back to the conversation that had sealed the deal. While Anne held on to her, still shivering, mulling over the dual but somehow conflicting prospects of extreme danger and freedom, Cristy was forced to recollect it more or less in its entirety to make doubly sure what she was about to do was the only thing left to do.

"I don't know what you're complaining about, Cristine. So you get disciplined once a month. You need it. Your sister will need it." Her mom's acerbic voice came into Cristy's head, setting her ears humming.

"It's not even that, it's just that it could happen anytime too." Cristy was moaning.

Her mom immediately cut her off, "Children need to learn how to behave. Besides, if you behave, you don't get punished, do you?" Her parents had initiated the threat of real punishment for most transgressions when she had become a teenager. Before that it was just spanking once a week or so. No big deal, she kept telling herself while it

155

was happening, and ten times over while it was happening to Anne. The thought of *that* had made her sick each time. How many times had she taken the blame for something in order to get her sister off the hook? It had only worked about half the time in any case. Most times, they both got it, and it was worse than usual because their dad suspected them of collusion. But for the past two years it had been the belt, and it was this that baby sister was now about to face as well. She had to put an end to it now or never. Her mom was still talking: "Kids think they should be able to do anything they want. Why? Adults don't get to do that. You need to learn that now or you'll never grow up." Cristy didn't bother responding. Besides, 'talking back' was one of the transgressions.

"I do behave myself," she stated shortly.

"And why? Because you don't want to stand up for dinner each day." Her dad had come into the room and had obviously overheard at least part of the conversation. Cristy quickly had to hide her look of disdain, no, hatred, that was threatening to flash across her face. She didn't look up at him as she walked hurriedly away out of the kitchen and down to the basement. It was the constant anxiety and not the actual scheduled discipline that had pushed her into this, she decided. She knew Anne felt it too and she thought that it was slowly eroding what little confidence her little sister had. Cristy had always been the one to talk back, the challenger. But Anne had seen the response and had never entered into the fray. Now it was time to step up, step out. Cristy came back to the present:

"Come on, angel-pet. We're sisters. Together we can do anything. Anything at all." Anne looked up, her face now damp. She snuggled in even more closely. Cristy could feel her fragile form, her budding bosom and tender thighs. She had to quit thinking about what they had done together last night in order to get on with the much more serious business of this afternoon. The two sisters held each other for a while and then Anne looked up, her face set more firmly.

"I'll do anything for you, Crissy. What do you need me to do?" Cristy tried not to sigh with relief. Then she tried not to dictate.

"I just need you to do what I said before. After dad's finished with you, get into bed and then wait a couple of minutes. Then get up. Don't put any other clothes on. Just your underwear. Go up the stairs and tell him you don't want to go to bed and you're not going to. It's far too early for someone almost thirteen. Whatever. Make something up to get him super-angry."

"He's gonna come after me."

"Which is exactly what we want."

"What if both strings fail?"

"Run out the back door and I'll improvise. Trust me." Cristy had thought of pushing the heavy planter that sat somewhat precariously on top of the back steps down on her father's head. It might well kill him, but it would certainly incapacitate him, perhaps for good. She would have to deal with her mom some other time, but there was just a chance that her mom, having to deal with either the death of her husband or his permanent head injury, might just deal with herself. That would be convenient, sure, but not as convenient as what she already had planned. It would be far better to see this immediate plan through. She gazed into her sister's eyes, smiling at her. Anne

157

might have faltered. "I love you, sis." Cristy's final reassurance, coming out of the night before was enough. Anne's face, momentarily paralyzed with the thought of her father's wrath, resumed its reflection of the life force, that same force her big sister's brain had been reflecting on for some weeks, though treating it as a problem to be solved.

Cristy waited until after lunch to set her lines, tying the thin nylon strings between the wooden balustrades while her parents were in their bedroom having sex. Woe betide any who would interrupt that, Cristy had found out, quite unwittingly a few months ago. She knew they wouldn't come out. But equally, when her dad finally did, Anne would, in her own way, be next up. Cristy even had the fleeting thought that the two acts were related. Had to be. Yes. That *was* it. Fucking pervert. She finished the top string, and stepping carefully over it, descended the stairs to the front door landing, then turned herself around and began to fasten the 'B' string to the top of the remaining flight. In some families maybe the father would actually get away with having real sex with the kids. Cristy guessed it depended on how sexy the mom was. Or at least, that had to be one of the considerations. Mom was still okay. She was super-thin. Almost as thin as the girls. Her face was pretty. She was a jerk to them, but that could only charm a man who demanded both obedience and loyalty from the entire household. Cristy finished up with a sigh of satisfaction. Anne was in their bedroom. It was up to her now. Then it would be up to Cristy again. Then it would be over. Cristy guessed that their grandparents would take them in. Time enough to plan that one out later. She climbed back up to the main floor and curled up in a corner out of the way.

Presently, her father sauntered out of the big bedroom. Cristy didn't have to look up to know exactly what was written on the bastard's face. Smug satisfaction about lust just passed. Gleeful anticipation about lust to come.

"Anne, get your butt up here right now!" he shouted down the stairs. He stalked back to the den. Now Cristy was sure it would work. He hadn't looked down at all, didn't notice anything amiss. And now she surely heard little sister's quiet footfalls on the stairs. Full of dread, no doubt. That feeling in the pit of your stomach. Cristy knew it well, of course. But it wasn't the actual physical thing that hurt so much as the fear, gnawing away at your insides. And yet this was supposedly normal. How fucked up the world was. It was time to change it. Cristy was feeling her own anger, and yes, even lust. She was going to enjoy it. Dammit, yes she was. She was trembling with anticipation. This was going to be her version of sex with adults. 'E' for excellent. 'B' for beautiful.

Anne was trembling too. They met each other's eyes from across the room, Cristy nodding her on. Anne's shivers were of course about something quite different. Their dad's heavy hand always made short work of her tiny posterior. If anything, what her parents thought was fair and normal for teenagers would be overkill for Anne all the more than for herself. Anne disappeared into the den, but it would be the last time. Cristy usually went outside when her sister was punished or sometimes hid in their bedroom and put earplugs in, but that was cowardly, she had recently decided. Though she recommended Anne do the same when it was Cristy's turn, today, of all days, Cristy knew she needed to listen to it happen, the whole thing. The tears, the girl she loved balling her head off, yelling and sobbing, the sharp smacks of calloused flesh upon that virgin, and her dad's vicious insults to boot. Was Anne - were either of them? – really a disobedient brat, a smart-mouthed bitch, a fucking slut-to-be? No. Anne was sweet. She was wonderful, tender, affectionate and giving. God, Cristy had found out just how affectionate just last night. And how desperately needy her baby sister was. She would do anything for her too. Anne's pledge of that morning rang in her ears, competing for a moment with the noisome lot of juvenile correction. What a stupid word. Pure rationalization. Nothing was being corrected here. Nothing put right. Her sister was being put in her place, but what place was that? Had she even ever left it? No. Anne was innocent, and would remain so. Her own conscience was clear, Cristy thought, and then swallowed hard. Her throat was dry and her eyes wet with empathy. But she needed to keep that down. Fury was the answer now. Controlled and directed, fury was the key to freedom.

The punishment finally over. Anne emerged, crying and red-faced, her own ears ringing with her father's "Get to bed! No nonsense either." 'Nonsense' probably referred to some version of what the sisters had begun together to explore last night. More unnecessary rules and restrictions. But no more asking 'when will it end?' Cristy nodded silently once again as Anne passed back down the stairs, and this, time, received a grim nod in return. Good girl, Anne! Cristy was elated. She moved into the dining room to get round back of where she expected her mom would reappear. Her father had come out of the den and settled down in the living room chair, flipping channels and breathing a little heavily. Cristy was out of his line of sight. It would just be a few moments now.

Though she could neither see nor hear her sister re-ascend, the fact it had taken place was violently announced by a growl from the vicinity of her father's leather recliner, and then: "What the hell are you doing back upstairs?" Now this was the moment, Cristy, sitting on the edge of her seat, couldn't breathe. 'Come on Anne, come on baby! You can do it, sweetie.' Cristy closed her eyes tightly, and then Anne's usually timid voice sounded out clearly and evenly across the room. "I'm not going to bed. It's too early. It's still light out. It's summer. There's no school in the morning." And so on. Cristy opened her eyes.

Then shut them again unwillingly at the sound of her father's roar. "That's just fine, missy. You won't be *able* to sleep by the time I'm through with you anyway. You see this? That's what you're about to get now, and get it good. Little bitch of a brat, I'll teach you respect if it takes all night!" No doubt her dad had been referring to the thick broad leather belt which adorned his oversized waist. It was a badge of office, a symbol of authority. He wore it, or something like it, almost every day. It was an emblem of dishonor even so. Cristy had felt it some thirty times already, and yet this was normal and accepted by most in their community. Her friends complained about it too, but did nothing. Whatever. It was fine to have rules. Cristy never wanted to hurt anyone. Doing her own thing didn't mean trespassing against others. No, this was about freedom. And love. Rules that impinged on those two things had to be broken. Authority that enforced those kinds of rules had to be stopped. And with a yell, a crash and a thump that shook the house, it had been.

Things happened fast now. Anne screamed and had apparently run back down into their bedroom. Their mom had rushed out of the master bedroom but Cristy was ready. By the time mom had reached the top of stairs Cristy was barreling in behind her. Mother's shriek at the sight of the lifeless body of her husband merged into a scream as Cristy, in the finest tradition of the broadcast left on in the living room, body-checked her down the stairs. The momentum carried Cristy forward but she was able to grab onto the balustrade and stop herself with a jerk. She hung there for a moment, and in that moment, her eyes met those of her mother's, staring, moving and trying to focus on her older daughter's face. Mom's lips tried with the greatest effort to frame the word 'why?', but just failed to audibly do so. Then it was gone. The life force, that is. Struck out of her mother's eyes, perhaps joining that which had been, moments before struck out of her father's. But in that moment, Cristy had felt the full horror of the scene.

She recovered partial equanimity by flicking the television off and nervously untying the top string from the two balustrades and shoving it into her pocket. She looked down and saw that blood had already spread itself all over the landing. It was slowly oozing from her father's mouth, but positively flowing from her mother's broken head. No going that way, Cristy thought.

"Anne! Anne, baby, it's all over.' Her voice was uneven. It must sound unsure to her sister. She took a deep breath. "Let me in the downstairs back door, will you? I need to get down to the basement, come up again and undo the other string, okay?"

"Okay," was all Anne was able to respond with. The timid mousy voice was back, but that would pass. Cristy took herself out the back and down the outside stairs. She had to traverse them with great care. What was that word? Ironic, that was it. It would be ironic in the extreme if she were now to hurtle down the stairs to her own fate given what had just transpired. Glancing back up at the unused planter, she waited at the door, resisting the urge to pound on it with all her pent-up anxiety. Nothing more than what was necessary must occur on her parents' property. Nothing to attract attention to themselves. A few moments of sweating and panting, in its own way not unlike the symptoms of what her and Anne had worked up to last night, and she was face to face with her new lover, the ashen face of her dear sister, adorned with desire but tarnished with need.

"I didn't look," was all she said, as Cristy passed back into the haunted house and wrapped her arms around Anne's shivering form.

"Don't. There's no need to. I'll get the other string. Get out my guitar and then I'll put these back on. Then we'll go out for a walk, come back by the front door. Discover them and go to the neighbours'. Then they'll take it from there and all we have to do is maintain our ignorance." Cristy emphasized each of these points with a squeeze and caress. "You can do that, can't you?"

"I didn't see anything. I didn't do anything." Anne was sobbing softly now.

"Right. Of course. But we need to go out for a long walk into the sea-breeze to get your face back to normal, huh?" Anne hadn't thought of that.

"Yes." Once again, a girl of few words. That was perfect for the task ahead, Cristy thought.

"We can't have anything looking out of the ordinary, know what I mean? People can't know you were just punished before this happened, or they might think to link it up in some way with us."

"I get it." Cristy kissed her on the forehead. With a little nod, Anne followed her to the foot of the stairs. You couldn't see anything from there. Cristy ascended, trying to ignore the wreckage that was coming into sight. She knelt down and undid the second string. It hadn't been necessary but you couldn't tell that ahead of time, could you, Cristy thought to herself. 'B' for 'back-up'. Guitar restrung, the girls headed out the back basement door and into the park behind the row of properties into which the now silent parental home had, for a time, receded.

****

The smell of hairspray. Gently jangling earrings, bangles, they were called, Cristy thought. Over-size glasses on an over-size nose. Was this the fourth or fifth office they'd been in today? The social worker was speaking to her:

"So your grandparents have agreed to take the two of you permanently?" Cristy was slowly coming back to the present. She felt Anne's grip tighten on her hand and she responded with a reassuring squeeze of her own. Where Cristy had just been was, if anything, more calm than the ministry office, with its sad eyes of neglect bursting into the sudden glare of morbidity. Desolation was an odor of the past, though, she told herself. She nodded. "After what you have witnessed and been through, I think this is the easiest solution. Otherwise it is likely you'd be separated." Another handwringing squeeze from Anne. Cristy nodded again. "We can check in with you guys regularly. I assume you like your grandparents okay?" Cristy could have but nodded again but was forced to pause. She didn't think much of them, living way out on that pathetic excuse for a farm, some miles from neighbors. She didn't trust them either.

But, she and Anne did have the advantage of being victims. There was credit aplenty in that role for now. It was a role that they had both played to a tee so far. After a pause, she nodded once again. The social worker raised her eyebrows: "Look, I know this is the toughest thing you two have ever faced. Losing both your parents on the same day to some freak accident...." Ms. Barnett, - that was her name; Cristy had forgotten it the moment she had introduced herself – Ms. Barnett cleared her throat, as if trying to remove some clotting bitterness associated with the words she had just uttered, and continued, "It's not an everyday occurrence. In my whole career here I've seen it rarely, always with a vehicular accident. Not with something like this."

That was an idea, Cristy thought, but it was too random to be effective. "But you're not orphans, you know, you still have family." This fact was, for the time being, convenient. Whether or not it would remain so well, only time would tell, thought Cristy, nodding again in the general direction of Ms. Barnett. "Is there anything else I can do for you at the moment, dears?" Ms. Barnett was now engaged in the struggle to insert some compassion into a bureaucratic process, always a tough sell. This time the response called for a quick waggle of the head, which Cristy accomplished and then looked at her sister. Anne did the same, her eyes staring blankly into the front of Barnett's desk. Cristy was proud of her, but a pang of conscience reminded her that this was not, for her sister, entirely an act.

Outside the office they waited in a glorious warmth of sunshine almost lost on them. Their maternal grandparents – thank god not their father's father, long dead and presumably well rid of - would take some time driving in from 'the farm' as they called it. Salt of the earth people. Cristy sneered. That meant their chief talent was akin to that of fertilizer. This then led to another, more interesting line of thinking. How old was her grandfather, anyway? Unexpectedly, Anne spoke, breaking in on her vague phantasm:

"I hardly know them. What are they like?" Cristy mulled it over. How much to tell and when was always the issue with a younger sibling. Not that Anne, once apprised, had ever let her down. Quite the opposite. But this time there might well be opportunities wherein her baby sister would not be called upon. It was her duty now, Cristy reminded herself, to keep Anne out of the line of fire whenever she humanly could. Anne was basically innocent. Any opportunity for the advancement of their shared dream should at its best, not besmirch her further. It was definitely a hurry up and wait situation, and Cristy, who felt inflamed by action, who felt its pull like nothing except the pull of Anne's warm tenderness, was unwilling to wait for too long. Yet at the same time, there was no apparent rush. Even so, Anne's question was very much her own. How much could they be themselves and still live with these new elders?

"Well, they're quite a bit older than our parents were. That's something important." Anne looked up at her sister with nothing but question marks riddling her face. "And... the place is in the middle of nowhere. We'll have to get a ride to school each day in the fall, about half an hour one way. But that could be something really important too."

"There's no bus?" Anne was obviously staying in the literal. Cristy's somewhat murky references were at the moment, lost on her. Well, she had only just turned thirteen.

"Nope." The district would not have been informed that there were now, suddenly, two teenagers living at the Parker Farm and not merely two people in their mid-seventies. "I'll learn to drive if I have to start on some dirty old tractor." At this Anne actually broke into a wane grin. Cristy grabbed her full and kissed her cheek a number of times. "My baby," she repeated. Anne cooed a little and nestled into her big sister's embrace. They held each other like that, turning the sympathetic heads of ministry personnel, single parents, and even some police officers alike. The police. Now *they* had been more observant than Cristy had expected. Maybe some of them were good at their job, she came away thinking after that little ordeal. It brought it all back, sitting there waiting for their grandparents to pick them up.

"So, you found your parents laying at the foot of the first flight of stairs when you opened the front door returning from a long summer walk?" the detective, a Mr. Atchison, repeated what Cristy had just said. She had nodded, but more alertly than in the social worker's office just now. She needed to be alert, she reminded herself.

167

"You were able to open the door all the way, then? To see inside?" Cristy waggled instead of nodding. Then she realized something needed to be said to clarify her story.

"Uh-uh. I had to peer around to see what was blocking it. I saw…" the detective put up his hand with a gentle gesture.

"It's okay, sweetie, you don't need to describe it." What Cristy had seen she had of course, already seen, but it was somehow different, coming back to them a few hours later, with Anne's face looking refreshed and normal and her backside able to help propel her gait in an effective manner. There was a lot more blood. So much that they had not been allowed back in the house since. A woman police officer had gathered what stuff they needed. She had asked them both to make a list, as long as they liked, she said. Their lists were long. They knew they weren't going back there anyway.

"I almost fainted. I kept Anne from looking in and steered her next door. I don't know how we even got there. It was like, all of a sudden you guys were there..." She let her voice trail off. The detective nodded and closed his eyes a little.

"It's okay," he said again. Of course, from his perspective, it wasn't okay at all. Not in the least. But Cristy didn't need to care about how he felt about it. She and Anne were rid of the first line of defense against freedom and love. What would the second line be like? She had abruptly returned to the present for a moment, but as there were no grandparents of any sort in sight, she lapsed back into her shadowy musing.

"We noticed a couple of things that maybe you guys might help us with?" Atchison was asking as gently as someone in his position could. Cristy wanted to help him. Of course, she thought, that was the best maneuver. Her eyes lit up in his direction and widened a little, anticipating a question. "Your mom was on her back. She somehow got turned around during her fall. This is unusual for that kind of accident. Was there something about her normal movement that might have precipitated that, like, did she often run around the house or, er…?" A pause, Cristy was wondering what he was trying to spit out. "Cristina, did you dad ever chase your mom around the house, like, even in fun and games, I mean?" Cristy thought of this for a second. What would be the best thing to say?

"We were out all afternoon. They told us to go out and enjoy the day because they had plans to do the same. I don't know what that entailed but they both seemed really eager for us to leave. Oh, it's just Cristine." Atchison looked inordinately embarrassed by not only what Cristy had just implied, but also that he might have added to her sense of alienation by forgetting her name a little, given the circumstances, of course.

"I'm terribly sorry, sweetie. Okay, so it might well have been that your parents were having some fun of their own in your absence. This might also explain why your dad's belt was unbuckled and loose around his waist when he was found?" Cristy had to do everything she could not to start or look scared. She managed it, barely. She had to blink a few times though, before answering. In that moment, she wondered how Anne would fare. They had asked the girls not to speak to each other in between the interviews, standard procedure, that sort of thing. Well,

Anne of course wouldn't tell the truth about the belt. That would be grievous if not necessarily fatal to their version of events. But it was how she would react that worried Cristy. The police blindsided you on purpose, she knew, just to gauge the truth quality of your reaction.

"I've no idea. I think they sometimes played rough, you know what I mean? I've heard them in the night once in a while. But, mom never complained about anything." Atchison was almost blushing. He sighed and went on.

"So what you're suggesting is that they could have fallen together, and ended up on top of each other, their embrace might have been loosened by the impact and your mother turned around?" Cristy was trying hard not to envision such a scene that never happened.

"I don't know." She shrugged, then closed her eyes. Not only for fuller effect, not only as a fulsome affect, but because she didn't want him staring into them for a time. She lowered her head as well. Atchison was on the point of giving up. There wasn't much he could learn from the kids in any case, he decided. They had said they weren't even there, basically for the entire afternoon. This was corroborated by the neighbours, as it was past five when the two girls had washed up on their doorstep, survivors of a wreck of titanic proportions.

"Thanks, sweetheart. We really appreciate all your help. It *has* helped, you know." He prodded gently. Cristy had now to look up and look him in the face. One final test. This accomplished, she was let out and, after giving Anne a warm hug of reassurance, the slightest nod in the affirmative, telling her that 'all is well', but not saying anything else, it was her turn to sit and wait. But Anne's interview was much more brief. Being the younger one,

Anne had used this to her advantage and simply threatened to break down any time the line of questioning became too murky for her to know what the best thing to say was. This was apparently much more heart-rendingly convincing even than Cristy's tack. How much of it was an act, big sister wasn't sure. The thought of her sister led her back into the present.

She squeezed Anne even closer and Anne responded by lifting her head up, now a little flushed, and, after kissing Cristy's ear, whispered, "I am so happy just to be with you now that it's all over." It wasn't over, of course, Cristy brooded. But this wasn't the time. In fact, allied to her nascent meanderings of some minutes ago, she once again took up the line of thinking that she might well be able to keep all further solutions from Anne completely and for good. She just might be able to, if she could get them separated. The distance between the farm and the nearest place where one could actually shop for more than food and farm equipment would probably do the trick. But it couldn't work until she could legally drive herself. That meant for another few months the two of them would have to more or less behave themselves. She needed that time anyway, not only to learn to drive, but to get the lay of the land, and, most importantly, to provoke in her grandfather feelings and their corresponding actions she already knew must be present in some form.

As if in response to her thoughts, her grandparents were abruptly upon them. A new, large pick-up with a rear row of seats had pulled up in front of the ministry offices. The oldsters had already disembarked and Gramma Jean was rushing over to them, her face a precious confusion of compassion and anxiety.

"Just look at the two of you, like foundlings on the doorstep! Come back home with us, your new home. Everything's going to be okay from now on, my dearest granddaughters." Jean was beginning to sob. That wasn't helping. At least, it wasn't helping her and Jerry, who had now worked his way over. He was still in good shape, though slower than anyone middle-aged. He was not perspiring from the effort of trotting over to them. Cristy was paying keen attention to all the relevant details. She made a pact-to-self to do so from now on. Jean had reached down for the both of them and they, in turn, gave her the requisite hugs and smallish smiles. Anne was still clinging to Cristy's arm, threatening to stop the blood flow. They ambled back to the truck and scooted in the back, still holding hands.

Gramma Jean continued without taking a breath, "Girls, we have beautiful rooms for the both of you, with beautiful views and beautiful beds and linen and…"

Cristy cut her off.

"We need to be in the *same* room, if you please, Gramma. Anne really needs me right now, as you can see." This stopped the effusive flow of Jean's *Wizard of Oz* welcome homecoming. But not for long.

"Of *course*, dear, of course. We'll move both beds into the bigger room then. We just thought that at your age, you might need your own space more, you know what I mean, we didn't think – we weren't trying to keep you apart. Goodness no." All this time Jerry's eyebrows had been slowly inching upwards, belatedly inclining themselves to follow his much more rapidly receding hairline. For the time being, however, he said nothing. "And we have an old armoire in the attic we could bring down if you need more closet space." At this, Jerry's composure almost broke its water. His face had turned just slightly carmine. But Cristy had not noted any heavier breath emanating from his chest and mouth. He turned for a moment and looked a little sharply at the girls.

"There's no boys within earshot of our place, you know," he stated flatly.

"We don't want any boys," Cristy returned, as flatly as she could manage, given this unexpected sortie. This appeared to rather please her grandfather, but then his look hardened once again and he started up,

"But we also don't expect the two of you to get up to any nonsense either." This untoward comment elicited a number of reactions. First and foremost, a cuff from Jean that sent Jerry retreating and fumbling around for some sort of apology, but just as importantly, Cristy, keeping her voice as even and dead-tone as possible, replied, "We're going to do what we need to do to recover from this, including sleeping together if Anne is frightened. If you don't like it, we can stay somewhere else."

Immediately Jean was off, "*Of course*, my sweet dear. The two of you have been through a horror, just a horror. You need each other. We won't do anything to keep you apart, will we honey?" This last comment was directed at her husband. He snorted a little but said nothing.

It was a long and dull ride from the coast into the interior. Dust, narrow roads, but no traffic. Three hours from their previous residence they rounded into the gravel access to their grandparent's farm, presently pulling up in front of a large old-fashioned looking farmhouse. Cristy thought it almost belonged on a film set. Anne had said absolutely nothing the entire time, lolling her side and head into Cristy's lap from time to time, never once letting go her grip on her arm. Jerry was Anne's older counterpart. Silent, a little morose. Brooding perhaps. People like her grandparents didn't really think about things, they ruminated, like their livestock. Their thoughts were the fuel for their fate, which Cristy had already adumbrated as that reserved for soil renewal. Jean carried on what was essentially a solo conversation the whole way back. Cristy wanted to tell her to 'shut it', as the old folks had it, but thought this out of character for the role she needed to play for a few months at least. How frustrating this waiting was going to be! But there was a time and a place for everything. What had already occurred had taught her that. She wasn't going to blow it now. The hard part was done, seemingly. Surely these two would be much easier to deal with than their own parents had been.

For starters, she was going to make sure there were no successful efforts, no efforts at all, to accost her and Anne in any way. She might have to wait for her moment to make this clear as well, but she had already scored a significant hit on Jerry's so-called morality by calling into play Anne's victimhood and fragile mental status, both of which were a stretch.

But only Cristy could know that. Anne's dolorous dropsy and her clinginess were not at all about her suffering, but more about the fact that since the event in their parent's house, they had not had a chance to love each other again. At one point during the ride to the farm, she had even gone so far as to bury her little nose in Cristy's crotch, under the guise of simply 'being close' and 'being afraid'. Cristy let her stay there for a little while, presumably breathing in the musky femininity of their shared youth. The night before their parent's removal had been a revelation for them both. Sure, they had played with each other, naked even, but not like that. They had been children together, and now they were something more, much more. Those youthful flames of ardor had once again caught fire in her little sister's breast.

But if they were to do anything about it tonight, in a brand new home, they would have to be much more discreet. Their new guardians never really went anywhere, least of all at night. The astonished squeals of delight, the moans and giggles, the joyous shriek that portended the paroxysm that had shook Anne's little frame from nose to toes, and the gratitude that had rushed from her precious lips that night two weeks ago or so could not be repeated anytime soon, no matter what chances they would have to reignite whatever else that had led to its birth. Silence in all things was their best bet for now.

They were all inside. Cristy was all business:

"I need you to teach me how to drive, Grammpa. Please. I saw your old truck outside. Does it still run?" Jerry blinked.

"You'll be sixteen when?" he asked dubiously.

"In about six months. If you prefer, I could start on a tractor." To this, Jerry just chuckled.

"No, the pick-up is fine. There's no place for city girls on farm equipment" Then his eyes narrowed in the manner that Cristy had seen back on the road. "You'll both stay away from the implements if you know what's good for you." The use of the stock and trade term 'implement' was interesting, Cristy thought. It was also a term that all sadists liked to use. The belt was an 'implement' to her dad, for instance. Out here it might be the leather strap. Who knew what lurked out in the barn or the various sheds that littered the back property? The place could be a veritable chamber of horrors. Cristy shuddered just ever so slightly. Another line of thinking she would have to keep from Anne as best she could.

Cristy nodded back, "Of course, won't go near them. I just didn't want to impose on you, that's all."

"The fact that you're both here is something of the sort anyways, isn't it," Jerry snorted back at her. It was significant that his wife was not within earshot. "I'll teach you how to drive. You need to look after yourselves out here. I've got a farm to run, and Gramma won't let me press girls into laboring on it. You can start younger than sixteen out here if you're just driving the two of you to school and back. Nothing else, mind you, or you won't be able to sit down and drive at all." Cristy knew exactly what he meant there. So it was as she had figured. Just like her father, Jerry sported a large band of leather around his relatively trim mid-section. Fuck him, she thought. Another chip off the old block. But that old block was not family, or even community. It was the whole goddamn society that was staring her down. She couldn't, she *wouldn't* bow her head to it, much less pray. She stared back at him.

"I can cook, clean, and wash clothes. Anne can do some of that already too. We're both okay students. We've never failed a class. We're both grateful to you and Gramma, really grateful." Jerry couldn't know how grateful, Cristy thought with some viciousness. Couple of doddering old idiots. It might take some time. Much more time given the laws of the land for her Gramma than for the pitiful excuse of a human being towering in front of her, but their time would come, nonetheless. "We're both *good* girls, too." She added with an emphasis she hoped would not be lost on him. That done, she turned on her heels and didn't look back at him. Her ears were turned back though. She couldn't possibly trust him. No, it was going to come to a head soon. Maybe the sooner the better. Well, tonight, by answering Anne's affectionate calls, they could frame the beginning of the scene. They could state their terms early on and dare their grandparents to do anything about it. Then both sides could maintain their distance. What had their history teacher called it? Some French sounding word: détente that was it. A mutually agreed upon apartheid.

But just like in history class, both sides would be looking for their opportunities. The best way to win that duel was to play into his hand as completely as she could, Cristy thought. Make him think that she needed what he thought she needed, and needed it badly. Then she would have him. Fuck yes, it was going to feel good. She could feel it in her heart already; the taste for action now outweighing the much more sophisticated palette of freedom. And this time she wouldn't really have to do much of anything. Not with him being so old. Not that he was frail. Oh no, no salt of the earth shit like him was going to go down easy.

All the better; he would over-reach himself and that would do him in. In an instant, Cristy already knew exactly what she was going to do. The question was, as ever, timing. And timing was, as ever, crucial. As soon as she had learned to drive. The first time after that, when her Gramma and Anne went shopping. That was the moment. Maybe a couple of months at most, just before school was due to resume. It needed to be done then. Then things could cool off until she was about to turn eighteen.

Upstairs to their now shared bedroom, Cristy found that her Gramma and Anne had themselves disassembled a second bed and were busy putting it back together again in a large and airy space. A fresh breeze was billowing out the diaphanous folds of the drapery. Cristy thought she would wrap herself naked in them and preen for Anne. What fun! The room was beautiful. Old-fashioned and feminine in the extreme. Furniture, linens, even curios from another time. A time when girlhood had been invented. Oddly appropriate, for this was now the time when it was about to be destroyed.

****

A huge welcome 'home' dinner. Cristy and Anne even dressed up for it, exciting the praise of Jean and the attention of Jerry. After all, she had coyly whispered to Anne when they were dressing, it would be all the more fun to undress each other later. Indeed, she had to fend her sister off whilst dressing up, the other's wondering joy so superabundant. Giggling, acting and looking for all the world like two youngsters without a care, they descended the long staircase to the main floor. Cristy smirked at it. Far too obvious to try that one again, though its length would have served admirably. Too bad. But not really. Her new ideas – plural, that is, for in the interim between helping set the room up and finding their clothing, she had charted out an end-game for her Gramma as well – were far more discrete and foolproof. Well, age and distance. Those two new factors made everything easy. Their only enemy was time. If it could be made into a simple companion, neutral, dispassionate, even uninterested, then even time could not act against them in the end. But how to do that part of it was still a little vague. Cristy fought back the urge to sulk about it. After all, the meal was excellent. No way she could have done it by herself. Gramma Jean was serving her purpose very well. For now.

Sitting there, trying to eat politely, the girls said little. They pretended to listen to news about 'the farm', or what summer was like in the valley compared to the seaside, and when it came to them being asked about what kind of food they liked, or what they wanted to do with themselves, or even what they needed to go back to school – a new school to boot – they kept their responses succinct and obedient. Cristy offered Jean her list of things she could do around the place. Gramma Jean was at first ready to refuse any help, saying that it wasn't the time for the girls to feel like they needed to do anything at all. Just have fun and enjoy the summer. All summer, that is, and then maybe when things calmed down they could help out during the school year. Just a little at first though. Jean was gently chiding them for even thinking about working. Her husband's eyes had that narrow look again. He clearly was more or less disgusted with his spouse. 'Things', as Gramma Jean had referred to them, must mean the girls' emotional well-beings. Well, Cristy had to accept that. She would have to be cool-headed. Hers was the infantry facing down the armour in an urban war. With the right techniques and weapons, a cool-headed infantry could almost always defeat a heavier opponent in that setting. Indeed, the rural was her urban, her fleet of foot would be her infantry, and her rhetoric her hand-held anti-tank stinger. The outdated heavy armour of her opponents would slow in time, find it hard to negotiate the twists and turns of youthful grace and apparent lack of conscience. The world was about to become hers. But no succession of power happened without a fight. There was something to be learned from history class, after all. The world had to be wrested from those like her parents and grandparents, in order for those like Anne and herself to take their rightful place. It was never a question of simple inheritance, Cristy had now realized, though that would play its not unimportant role later on as well.

Dinner over, the girls cajoled their Gramma into letting them clean up and even wash and 'put things up', another oldster favourite. "Okay, but just this once for now," Jean chided. "Such good girls," she continued to Jerry as the two of them retired to the gigantic living room, turning on the television. Hockey again, Cristy noted with a smirk. It would be more apt this time around, she opined to herself, if it were the Olympics, but it was the wrong summer for those. Dishes and kitchen cleaned spotless, the girls begged to be excused given the travails of the day. Only this morning had they finally rid themselves of the pesky social worker assigned to their 'case'. What case? Cristy had questioned, in a moment of indiscretion. But it was a mere categorical term, with no fuller meaning or intent. She had then shrugged along with the process, lasting for days and days. They were put up in a motel, with careful oversight. The system had been trying to live down a scandal involving placing wards of the state in cheap motels, to hob-knob with hookers, and for some, to join with them in various ways. A more or less shitty time, though they could in fact do whatever they wanted in the motel suite after the last social worker had checked on them, just before their curfew. And they had done something, at least. Not to the extent of the first time, but enough to get them through the intervening period of anxiety and fear of the unknown long-term. But it was somehow dirty, there, in the smelly motel with its porous walls and its distracting clatter. It didn't feel the same. Both naked and sitting on the bed within reach of each other, Cristy recalled looking at Anne and then the both of them bursting out in nervous laughter at it all. We might as well have been hookers too, Cristy had thought. If it weren't for their grandparents, Cristy had wondered if they might well have gone down that road eventually. A little sting of conscience, then it was gone.

Upstairs, they were in each other's arms, fawning, caressing, then kissing. Both of them inept but good natured about it, they danced how they imagined lovers might dance. They undressed each other, flinging the precious vestments hither and thither, making the Victorian room seem even more like a boudoir. Cristy then grabbed the viscous sheen of the under-drapes and wrapped herself inside, giving her little sister her best smile. Anne was entranced. She approached her big sister with gentleness and reverence both. They ended wrapped right up together, and then with a crash, on the floor, all tied up in a bundle of drapery that had come off the vault above the high, long window simply because they had been fooling with it, and their combined weight took it down. But they laughed and laughed, even though when they looked up into the face of their Gramma and saw for an instant the same stern judgement that their grandfather

181

never attempted to hide, they had to immediate lapse into the meekest apologies and promises to 'never do it again'. For her part, Jean recovered with some grace, and after that instant her face was back to the 'Gramma' of sentimental script. But the reality was still clear enough for everyone. Jean and Jerry were far too old to be saddled with raising a couple of energetic teenagers. It wasn't fair, and even though they could not know that it also hadn't been really necessary either, at least from the point of view of most adults in the area, even Cristy had to admit to herself that she would be more or less shortly doing them a favour. She had not, up until that moment, thought of this further rationale. But because it put her grandparents into too good a light, and maybe also inserted a slice of reality into the whole thing, she decided she wasn't going to lean on it all too much.

As they were struggling to disengage from both each other and from the drapery, Jean sidled backwards toward the door, then spoke. "You girls try not to wreck the place, would you? I guess you're both glad to be safe and all. Staying in that sleazy motel must have been terrifying for you. I am so glad that you're back to acting your age after all this grown up stuff." That was how she rationalized what she had seen. Oh, god, the things people had to do to avoid the truth, Cristy thought as she sat up on her haunches, not wanting to display her young womanhood to an old woman. Cowardice was everywhere in their world. Hip – what was that word again? – hypocrisy, she thought. It's always hip to be a hypocrite, she sang to herself as she helped Anne disentangle the last vestiges of drape. Anne then surprised both her and her grandmother by dancing up, spinning around and grinning at them. This forced Jean, mouth agape, to beat a hasty retreat back out the bedroom door, mumbling something about 'getting it fixed in the morning'. The sisters then tried to keep from laughing as they shut the door. There was no lock. Well, why would there be in this old place? Cristy thought. She shoved a heavy chair in front of the door. "Just for now," she added to Anne, who looked on approvingly. "No more interruptions." Brushing aside the fact that it had been their own mischief that had brought their grandmother upstairs in the first place, they continued their dance. After a time, they fell into one of their beds in a languorous heap. What followed brought the two sisters together in a new way once again, and afterwards, Cristy had to apologize for covering Anne's mouth up rather forcefully during the climax of the scene. Anne blinked at her big sister and smiled. "Who cares?" she whispered. Then, "Wanna do it again?"

Cristy had no idea when they had fallen asleep, but upon awakening, it was already quite bright in their room, the fallen drapery accounting for much of this delightful expression of the young summer, eager to add its love to the mix already begun by its poorer cousins, the human youth. Anne was still sleeping. Cristy resisted the urge to jump on her, or even to pet her. Anne needed to sleep. In fact, Cristy now uttered a little prayer to the new world that asked of it that Anne should sleep through the next few years, not literally of course, but metaphorically. Should sleep through what Cristy was going to do and only then wake up at the other end. And today? Today, was but the 'end of the beginning', another quote from history class. Even so, and akin to that much greater conflict all those years ago, fought by the same people that now needed to *be* fought, Cristy could imagine the real end, and set herself to accomplishing it with all due speed.

****

"Now there's no clutch. You just put this lever here, and then you step on the gas with your right foot. Here, you can see on the steering hub these letters, right? 'R' for reverse. 'D' for drive', 'N' for neutral. Neutral isn't a gear, you don't go back or forward with it. It's just there to save the transmission."

Cristy nodded attentively, though she had to shake off a momentary memory of other letters and what they had stood for. 'F' for focus, girl, she told herself. Fucking focus and fuck the rest of it for now. Her guitar was in the other room, abandoned at night but used aplenty during the odd rainy day. It was grand to have both a huge bedroom and a slightly smaller play-room for them both. Her guitar was slowly getting better, playing for Anne, who lapped up every note of it, sitting at her feet, the sweet thing. But goddammit, focus!

Jerry's bullish rattle continued, "Now that you're in reverse, just hold the wheel straight and press down on the pedal. That's it, girl, back it out." The old truck groaned and lurched. Its chrome flapped in the breeze. It had no tail-gate, and the bed was covered with rust. The cab was not too bad, though Cristy could smell stale tobacco and mildew. But it ran. In fact, her grandfather had been using it up until a few months ago, when they had finally been convinced to buy the huge new vehicle that had, according to Jerry, turned heads down in town. Some town, Cristy mentally withdrew a sneer. But this old thing would get them to school and back, as well as to the local grocers and market. That was good enough. The thing now was to learn to pilot it. Like any courtship, you had to gain an understanding of what it would and wouldn't do for you, just like with people. Well, except for her and Anne, that is. They knew they would do anything for each other. Well, they had already proven that, hadn't they?

Then, 'FF' for 'fucking focus'. Cristy closed her eyes tight for just a moment, and then cleared her mind. The scent, no, the smell of her grandfather was making her a little nauseous. But that's what you had to expect. Shit smelled, and there was nothing you could do about it while it was still above ground.

"Now, put the lever in 'drive', and push down on the gas a little. While you do that, turn the wheel to the left and pull out of the yard." Cristy was all business, accomplishing this minor feat without delay or demur. "Good girl." Jerry reached over and squeezed her shoulder and rubbed her neck a little. Oh, holy fuck, it's starting already, is it? Cristy thought. And fuck me, the old fart's touch felt good. A litany of curses started to spring up in the fertile soil of her unconscious. They were keen on reminding her of their undergrowth, always present but suppressed. This is why families didn't really work, thought Cristy. This is why parents beat their kids. This is why young people replaced parents with lovers, so she had heard in her introductory psychology class. No doubt the rural high school would have no such elective. Fuck me and fuck him, she added to this otherwise fairly sound analysis. Well, I will. She herself caressed this thought, turning it over in her hands, making it feel wanted in the same way that she made Anne feel like she was the only person in the world. All the while she had been driving, albeit slowly, and finally, glancing out of the windows, started a little at just how far down the gravel lane they'd gotten.

"Yup, you ought to look out of the windows once in a while, there, Cristine," was her grandfather's retort to her brown study.

She gave him the patent sheepish smile, part, 'I know I'm a naughty girl and an airhead', and part, 'please forgive me'.

It was astonishing, even to her, how rapidly one learned these scripts, and just how effective they were in the world of adults. Was that because adults simply were that stupid? Or did they know the truth of things and conspired to cover it up for convenience? Cristy couldn't quite tell which was which, or whether or not it was some of both, or maybe something else, even. For now, she needed to retain the controlled passion of the pragmatist, and above all, focus on the task at hand. She seemed to be making progress. Jerry was as complimentary as he could possibly be, she thought. All too complimentary, as his hand had inexorably slid over to her shoulder once again and was massaging it, while he was encouraging her verbally to 'mind the lay of the road' and 'plan ahead for all possible turns', or even darting animals. And Christ, she was starting to get aroused now. Cristy closed her eyes again, this time just for a moment too long, for she suddenly felt her grandfather grab the wheel and turn it sharply away from whatever had gotten in their path. She almost instinctively hit the brake. Jerry looked like he was about to tear a strip off her, probably quite literally wanted to. But she wasn't going to be a coward. She turned and faced him.

"You were distracting me. Touching me like that. I can't drive with that going on. Maybe some other time," she added, delighted to have the opportunity to begin her ambuscade. Her grandfather's attitude had turned from anger to a quizzical anticipation.

"Alright. I don't know how it is with young folks. Kids and the like. One moment it seems you need to be hugged and the next moment whipped. I can do both, of course." He didn't quite menace. "Just stating the facts as I see 'em," he finished.

Cristy was not at all surprised. That's what adults basically were. One part lascivious lecher one part surreptitious sadist. Usually it only got obvious during the teenage years, and especially with girls. She and Anne were, apparently, most at risk according to the statistics that they'd been showered with during their copious visits to social services. Anything like that they needed to report, of course, and all this was in preparation for what the ministry had assumed was to be foster care. When their grandparents had stepped forward, at the tenth hour, the stats had been shelved. How naïve.

"I'll let you know when I need either of those, thanks," Cristy said, keeping the malice out of her voice. Then, "And I know I'll need them both." She herself reached over and patted her grandfather's knee, giving him a little smile of contrition. For his part, Jerry's eyes widened significantly. He settled back into the seat with a satisfied grunt, then told her to 'get driving' again. Cristy took her time, she wanted to learn as much as she could each practice run so she didn't have to spend any more time in the cab of the old truck with Jerry as she possibly had to. Even so, this first lesson was paying dividends at a number of levels. Things were going exactly how Cristy wanted them to go. Even her own reactions to the old man's ministrations could help the cause. It would make her even more convincing when the time came. Of course, none of this would ever reach Anne's ears let alone her eyes. And Cristy would never let the old shit go too far, get too near her. For all that, it was even possible she had grossly misinterpreted his intents anyway. He was a bastard, sure, but he didn't seem like a pedophile. *What* was she thinking? He had basically told her she needed to be punished, and severely. Well, that alone was enough, wasn't it? That was the same thing as sex anyways. She had already figured that out weeks ago now. The 'implements' might be a little different, but all of them were basically a replacement penis. A prosthetic phallus, to be more exact, though Cristy couldn't possibly have worked that out. Someone like her grandfather would need it not just because of what society had to say about adults and kids and intimacy, but because he literally couldn't get his real cock to do the job anymore. In this, at least, he was much less dangerous than her father might have been.

They returned the way they had came. "Good first time, girl, I'm impressed."

"So you don't need to take me out behind the barn just yet, then?" she queried as sweetly as she could in return.

"Not yet." He smiled back at her.

Fuck him. That'll be the day, Cristy thought, and it *would* be, she then added to herself with a silent laugh. It fucking would be. She reported to Anne how she had done, trying to avoid having to spend a couple of hours with Gramma as she prattled on about nothing.

Anne was interested in something different, however, "What are you going to do about them?" This knocked Cristy flat aback. "Big sister, I *need* to know so that I can help you." Cristy was lost for words for a time. This was totally unexpected and of course, didn't fit at all with anything she was dreaming up.

"Listen, baby girl, please, not this time. Let me look after it. You've done enough. It's not right that you should have to go through this." This shit, she thought, but she always tried not to curse in front of Anne. Her little sister was, in fact, the only person she extended this grace to, though now that they were ensconced in their grandparents' house she had stopped cursing completely, at least for the time being. She didn't want her grandfather to get the jump on her for any reason, any excuse to blindside her and take her down early. She knew from bitter experience that it took several days to recover from real discipline. During that time her energy level and movement would be impaired. She would not be able to run as fast. She wouldn't be able to rest in the usual way. Her sleep would be troubled and her rear end would be sore as hell. There was no way around it. The only time she could let him have even a foretaste of it was when she needed him to. Having Anne in the mix would complicate matters to the nth degree. "You've got to stay out of trouble here, okay, angel?" Anne blinked at her, seemingly without understanding. "I mean it, my pet, my best girl, you've got to do everything you can to make sure Grammpa doesn't punish you. I can't stand in for you right now, I guess that's what I'm saying."

"If he wants to whip me then I'll take it. You're *not* going to take it for me any more. There was enough of that before." Anne was uncharacteristically adamant, as well as showing impressive pluck. Cristy fairly leaped on her and pushed her to the bedroom floor, whereupon they kissed and kissed again. Cristy found herself tearing up.

"*No* and *no*. That's all over now. Neither of us is going get it here. I just need you to be a mouse in the house for a few more weeks, okay? Don't ask me about it, don't try to help me. Help out the old woman if you need something to do when I'm not around. I'll be watching over you. Grammpa won't get near you. But at the same time, don't give him any excuse. I need to be fit and ready, well rested, okay?"

Cristy was now almost ready to start slobbering over her kid sister's face, but Anne had grown all the more tender during this little diatribe, and reached up, caressing all the tears away, and even licking them off Cristy's cheeks, all the while saying, "I love you, big sister. You're the best. I want you every day. I want to live with you forever and ever." And after these and related sentiments, Anne got suddenly serious and stated, "Crissy, my hero, if he hurts you, if he starts it, don't let him end it." Cristy looked Anne right in the eye and said firmly:

"Don't worry, I won't."

****

The intervening period of days and then weeks took up some semblance of a routine. Cristy was surprised at her acumen for driving, she even actually liked it. It was the lighter side of her self-realization that balanced out the shadows of having to face the fact that she also liked her grandfather's touches and even got off on his thinly veiled threats. And she realized that in some other age, in some other community, her actions and even her thoughts would warrant a regular thrashing of ritual proportions. This too played its part in her connivances, her theater, and her passivity in the face of Jerry's on-rush of simultaneous accusation and desire. But having experienced a few too many real whippings – and what the hell was she saying, *one* was too many – at the hands of her late father, she knew that all of this was but a juvenile fantasy. Even so, it served her purpose, allaying her once palpable fear of having to actually go through the possible risks involved in what was day by day, getting closer and closer to her. When the time finally came, about six weeks into the summer, she felt like she was ready. She and Anne had avoided any insult, up to and including outright assault. Jean was the picture of hospitality, and even Jerry was more or less only gruff, rather than at all violent. And so it came to pass that on the day appointed, one of Jean's local friends and her young nieces trundled both Jean and Anne off to the city for a day of real shopping. Jean was almost shocked when Cristy had elected not to go along.

"There's plenty of room in the van, dear. I just don't understand why you'd want to stay home on a day like this!" Cristy has assured her Gran that she would have wanted to go to altogether different stores than would the younger girls. This was not really true of course, but no old person would ever know the difference. They said their farewells. Anne gave her a long hug and an even longer look in the eye. They said nothing, however.

Waving them off, Cristy turned and almost bumped into her grandfather, who had ostensibly been doing the same thing.

"Sorry, Grammpa. Didn't know you were right behind me," she said a little nervously. Jerry patted her shoulder and said

"Why don't we go inside. I feel like I hardly know you after all this time. My fault. I think I've come across as an old grouch. I'm the one who should be apologizing." So far so good, thought Cristy. She followed him into the living room and sat down opposite him, far enough away that he could not reach for her without getting up. Just enough distance to make a run for it when the time came. Cristy made sure the back door was open. "Why don't you take your shoes off and relax for a while. What did you say you wanted to do when you grew up, anyway?" Cristy was not about to begin *that* sort of inane conversation. The kind of thing old people wanted to hear from young people. That they had accepted the lie and were going to not merely go along with it but support it wholeheartedly; jobs, marriage, families, kids, schools, governments, wars. Cristy had her own war to wage. Jerry was just now entering her sights.

"I thought I'd go for a run later on," said she, wiggling her feet at him. She had on more or less new athletic shoes. They each weighed about as much as a feather. She eyed Jerry's tired boots and tried not to smirk. She had on her track shorts and top, which to any eye older than maybe thirty would be seen as a disgrace, fit only for a street-walker in a city of sin. Their abbreviated quality also, however suited her designs to a tee. She knew how she looked in them. Just about an hour ago Anne had caught her preening in the mirror. Anne wanted to get into bed with her that moment, but Cristy begged off, promising a lot more tonight than was usual even for them. For tonight, for the first time, she thought they could count on being alone in the big old house. Her grandfather nodded. "I thought I might need to run off some soreness, you know, in some muscles."

Jerry was actually on the point of losing interest. She obviously had to come right out and say it. And after a deep breath during which she counted to ten in her head, she did: "You said something in the truck the first time we did a driving lesson, remember, about disciplining me if I thought I needed it?" Now she had his attention back. "Your Gramma's second husband, right? I think she is still in mourning about what happened, I mean, we all are, but you maybe not quite as much? I just need to clear my head, get some focus back for school, start practicing track and all."

She gestured at her attire. He was looking at her up and down, insofar as he could given she was still seated, but indeed, now on the edge of her seat. "I thought maybe you could help me out with getting back some focus about the here and now, preparing for the future, that sort of thing?" She was using her meekest, most little girl voice. Jerry was now all ears. Finally! But there were none of the other necessary signs. No furrowed brow, no snarling lips. No narrowing of the eyes, a key sign with her dad that something dangerous was about to transpire. She kept at it: "You *can* do that, right? You weren't just blowing hot air at me, or were you?" Now there was the slightest shadow that Cristy could see slowly spreading across Jerry's visage. But there was a ways to go yet, she knew.

"I certainly can, young lady. I don't blow hot air, by the way. What are you suggesting?" he replied, studying her but without moving. He was just starting to get surly.

Cristy was, however, just starting to get nervy. But she was quick to swing it up a few notches, after all, this whole thing was but a prelude:

"So here's your chance to put your money where your mouth is, old man. I need you to go get your strap, or whatever you use for a penis, and give it to me good and hard. Maybe out behind the barn. That's the old tradition, isn't it, amongst people like you?"

This broadcast got Jerry out of his chair, but she had been waiting for this. More quickly than he ever could, she was up and out the back door, stepping off the porch onto the hard ground of a hot summer. This was one more variable in her calculations, and a relatively important one at that. He fairly stormed out after her, but stopped on the porch. She would have to draw him off.

"Your mouth is one thing that needs adjusting," he stated baldly. He was fingering his belt. He must have been wondering if she was going to run for it. If so, he would have to leave his belt on to keep his pants from impeding his progress. But Cristy could see that he was still far too rational for her plan to ever come to the necessary conclusion. She stood there cockily jeering up at him, and started in again: "So, you know, uh, 'Gramps' – by the way, that's what they're gonna call you in prison; I hear prison's pretty dull but you're gonna be the life of the party. You know how they treat child molesters in prison, don't you? Boring stuff, but now 'Gramps' is here, every night is a good night..." She broke off because he was now coming straight at her. Jeez, he could move way faster than she had thought! But hardly fast enough, Cristy was off in a flash, increasing her lead without over-exerting herself. He doggedly pursued. Now he was getting angry in the serious way she needed him to. She increased her lead and then turned and faced his rush. He pulled up too, thinking that she would just take off again. Instead, he opted for the obvious ruse of slowly inching up on her position, as if she would fall for that. "So, like I said, Gramps, I think I need a dose of your medicine if you're man enough to give it to me. How old are you, anyway? Bet you're starting to feel it now, huh? Anyway, I wore these shorts just for you, or, should I say, for your stand-in. They're not going to offer much protection against your 'implement', are they?" he started to advance upon her with a roar. She turned and once again easily attained a safe distance. Behind her she heard him yell.

"No, they're not! I'm going to enjoy seeing you beg for mercy after a dozen licks, you little brat. But that'll just be a warm up." Cristy thought she might have heard him give his first gasp. Good sign that, but like her history class said, this might only be the end of the beginning. She continued to trot out ahead, leading him towards the old barn. Whatever he was going to use on her must be located inside there, handily, at least in the old man's perverse fantasy, because no one, quite apart from the school bus system, could have predicted the sudden appearance of two teenage girls on the old farm. She was using about half her pace, she thought. He was starting to gain on her, amazingly. But he couldn't have the reserve power she had. She called out at him again, "I can't wait to feel it, Gramps. I really need it bad. Take all the time in the world. I don't want to sit down for a month. I like standing up anyway."

Cristy's problem was now becoming more clear. It had nothing to do with the physical and everything to do with the fact she was running out of insults to hurl his way. It was starting to become a farce. She needed to think faster than she needed to run to make this work. She realized she needed to take a bigger risk to put him over the edge. Another deep breath and another ten count. 'C' for 'courage', she said to herself. Then, as she turned round the back of the barn, she stopped dead. Breathing only a little more heavily than normal, she waited for him, casting her head around to make sure there were suitable places of exeunt. But he did not immediately appear. What the hell was he doing? She made sure of the approaches. He was not coming up from behind her, nor was there any cover behind the barn. No bushes to pop out from, no depressions in the surrounding landscape into which one could lower oneself, if he even had that kind of flexibility, which she seriously doubted. Then she wondered if her desired outcome had already occurred. Now *that* would be a bonus, but she didn't trust it. She thought he had sidled up against the wall of the barn that faced away from her, and was simply waiting for her to peer around it. Another old trick that she wouldn't ever fall for. That must be what he's doing, Cristy thought with a sneer. She backed away from the building to get an even better view of the approaches. Even at thirty paces or so the ancient barn towered over her. Its presence felt ominous. This wasn't where her mom had grown up though. But somebody had, a lot of somebodies. And those somebodies must have been marched out here to take their whippings on a regular basis, maybe every Sunday after church. That would make sense, given the corrupt and perverse nature of these people's beliefs. Cristy was starting to get distracted. Jerry might think to rush out suddenly from one of the two angles hiding her view of the sides of the barns that faced away from her.

But she was wrong, totally and completely, for there was a rustle overhead, and a fair thud to her left. She started and yelped a little, looking up. A door in the second story of the barn was open, but there was no one in its frame. And yet, as she cautiously approached the object that must have emanated from this door, thrown almost at her but carried off its intended trajectory by its liquid shape, she suddenly froze in her tracks. Lying on the ground was a wide, heavy leather strap complete with a wooden handle. Cristy's knees started to shake a little. This would never do. He's trying to scare me, distract me from being able to keep up the chase, she realized. But it was starting to work. She couldn't get any closer to the horrible thing. It looked well enough used, but still obviously supple. Its very suppleness had prevented it from coming right down on top of her. He had gone into the building, found just what he was looking for and announced it in an unexpected way. Now, she could have simply picked it up and ran with it, maybe throwing into the farm pond where he couldn't possibly get at it.

But she couldn't even get nearer than a few meters, let alone pick it up. It might be an oversize poisonous snake. It *looked* snakish. And snakes had a temper. Her grandfather's temper was meant to be transmitted into that implement. It was like an electrical wire. Its end would touch her flesh and burn it. She would start to scream if he managed to hit her more than a few times with something like that. Jesus, where in hell would he have even gotten it? Some artifact from an antique prison? She would scream under its tenure. But she knew that's what he wanted, her screaming. Her body was now shivering a

197

little. She needed to get a grip, and quickly. He would know, or at least guess, that the sight and presence of something like that might well cow a youngster. He might think that the girl would stay put and expect some mercy rather than carrying on and delaying the inevitable. Yeah, that would have worked if Jerry had been in his prime. After all, she might tire even a younger man out but she would, in the end have to submit because there was nowhere else to stay. He could drag her out of bed in the middle of the night, march her back here, and nigh-on kill her with that thing. She had to avoid looking at it.

Pay attention only to the approaches now. This was a crucial moment. She still had the advantage if she could maintain it. Jerry was, in fact, *not* a man in his prime. She could run rings around him and he could do nothing. But she still needed him to chase her as long as possible, and he only would if he was angry enough to lose all control. He obviously wasn't there yet, and this latest ruse had proven it. Only a rational mind would think of scaring her into submission beforehand. She was shaking a little more, realizing that she had to basically place herself close to his mercy and only then, at the last second, betray him and his perverted lust. *That* would set him off. Hopefully it would be enough.

Then he appeared, quite suddenly and without warning, from around one side of the barn. He stalked towards her.

"I see you're starting to behave yourself. Well, maybe we can take that into consideration a little later when you're on the ground begging for me to stop, eh?" he had reached the place where the horror lay. He had no scruple about picking it up and brandishing it. He flicked it once and to Cristy's ears there was almost a report, a small explosion. He was trying to scare her, freeze her into immobility. Goddammit it was almost working! She hadn't expected either his tactics or her reaction to them. Fuck him. Fuck this. Cristy was breathing hard now and not at all due to any physical exertion on her part. Her knees were moving again. Of course he noticed as he came in closer.

"This is going to change your life, missy. You're never going to forget it. Like all good medicine, the dosage can be repeated if necessary. I think you're in for a regular dosage over the next few weeks. I think you know you need it. By god I'm gonna make you beg, you sorry brat. You're already shaking like a leaf. Just wait until I straighten you out, you're not going to be even able to walk, much less run like a deer."

He was inching in closer and closer. She was frozen now. Her breath was rapid. She knew that it was over unless she could shake herself out of it right now. He wanted to hurt her in a serious way. This was not going to be anything like even what her dad had done to her. This thing in her grandfather's grip was more than just an instrument of 'correction', it was a weapon. In the hands of a determined and furious man, it might be close to lethal. But more than that, this man was interested, nay, would take the greatest of delight in torturing her, a lithe young girl. And it was something that had been going on for millennia. It had much of the weight of public opinion behind it to this day in certain areas. It was *more* than perverse, it was….it was…*oh my god*, he's only a couple of meters away now!

Cristy finally got it out of her, shouting the word at the top of her voice, "EVIL!!"

This scream had the dual effect of releasing her from the gaze of that very thing which had been hunting her down, as well as stopping Jerry in his tracks for a moment. That moment was all she needed. She raced off with him giving the hottest pursuit he could. He was himself screaming back at her, but she couldn't make out what he was saying now, as the distance between them increased. She vaguely heard something about not being able to walk, about never even looking at him the wrong way again, or some other utter nonsense. And now he seemed very far off indeed. Cristy finally dared to turn and look. Jerry had stopped. He no longer had the strap in his hand. That would be handy later on, Cristy thought, her rationality gradually flowing back into her still supercharged sensibilities. He had slowed considerably. Cristy let him get back within hailing distance, whereupon he began to echo some of her earlier thoughts:

"You have to come back to the house sometime, you sneaking little bitch. I'll haul you out here in the middle of the night. I'll make you wish you never were born. I'll march you out here and whip you naked for an hour. You won't be able to think let alone talk when I'm done. We can do that once a week and see if you still want to disobey me!"

He was slowly advancing upon her position, but without the scheming sense of the tactician he had almost successfully parleyed into her demise before. He was also breathing quite heavily and his face was an ever-deepening red. Cristy knew she was getting there. She was back in the moment now, focused, ready to finish this off. They were nowhere near the barn, the horror had been left to rusticate on its lonesome somewhere back out behind them. She would have to find it and put it back where it had been, or secure it in some other way so that it could not ever be found. She hadn't quite decided on the best course of action for that yet. She felt a renewed sense of purpose, and with it, that of confidence as well.

She hollered back at him, "Dream on, old man. Look at you, you're nowhere near being able to lay one lick on me. It'll never happen and you know it. All that hot air — what it's doing for you, giving you a hard on? I bet you fall asleep at night dreaming of whipping beautiful young girls until they're half dead, and then maybe raping them to boot."

Jerry was almost at a standstill, he was breathing so hard. This had gone on long enough, Cristy decided. She abruptly changed tactics yet again and ran straight at him, bearing down on him, her face grim. He started back a little, then came towards her at his best remaining pace. They would meet in seconds. Cristy waited until the last possible moment and then altered course, brushing by him too quickly for him to grab her. But not just brushing. As she passed him she flung a fist into his solar plexus as hard as she could. The impact almost took her arm off as she raced by, but he was on the ground, groaning. Round one to her. She set her face again after letting herself have the luxury of a momentary smirk. She turned and raced by his prone form, stomping on his outstretched hand as she went by. He yelled out, cursing her to the devil. Fine, she thought, the devil has to be more challenging than you, you turd. She turned again, but he had had enough and was up and moving towards her, doubled over a little, with one arm laggardly slung by his side. She trotted out ahead but now he had lost control.

This was the climax, Cristy thought. She did a quick scan of herself and her surroundings. No physical injury, lots of physical energy left. Lots of space around her to maneuver. Fair distance back to the house. Path wide enough to get around him if he got too close. But mentally, she realized she was almost spent. She needed to finish this and finish it soon. She was just able to focus. 'F' for focus, double 'f' for you know what. She repeated this to herself a few times while he bore in on her. She turned and started to run at a decent clip. The ground was even, hard as rock given the summer season. Her laces were still tied tight. Such as they were, her clothes were still on. Her clothes! By god, *that* was it.

She stopped dead. Tore off her top and turned around. "Hey old man, isn't this what you wanted to see?" She then slipped out of her running shorts, 'buns' as the girls on the track team called them, for obvious reasons. Once again she waited almost too long and threw the two items almost in his face, now upturned to check his progress, now turned to the ground in response to his breathing. The sight of this nascent naked wisp of womanhood almost stopped him again, but he soldiered on with a growl and some more nonsense like 'now you're ready for the whipping of your life, young lady'.

She jeered at him, "I've been ready for hours now and nothing's happened. You know what a girl needs, that's for sure. What a winner. Sorry honey, but you're not getting a second date!" With that Parthian shot, she herself shot off ahead of him, back towards the house. He was really dragging now, his fury had consumed him and

202

it appeared to be the only thing left that was keeping him going, They were nearing the back yard of the farmhouse when it finally happened. Cristy heard a dull thud somewhere behind her and a heavy groan, then silence. She stopped and turned. Nothing. Was this another ruse, a last minute desperation? She waited long enough to gain full possession of her physique, then waited a little longer to gain some small possession of her rationality and common-sense, then started back down the path, walking this time. Almost immediately he came into view, what was left of him. In a heap on the dry dusty parched ground of his world had he expired. Coming up on him cautiously, she could now see it was no ruse. Blood had spurted from his mouth and nostrils. His injured hand would be put down to his fall, as would any bruising of the abdomen caused by her run and gun attack. The thing was done. Cristy didn't need to set her face; the satisfied smile that had appeared upon it was as genuine as the death that brazenly exhibited itself in front of her.

****

The warmth of the sun felt so good on her naked body. This was a freedom too, she thought. She was alone. That too was unexpectedly liberating. Not even Anne was needed, just at that very moment. It was a moment she would savor then, taking it all in. She had cut a wide swath around the corpse. Flies were already buzzing at the bloody face. She paid them no attention and the body only the attention that such a thing deserved. She retrieved her clothing but did not immediately dress.

She trotted on back towards the barn, her eyes now on the alert for the Thing itself, the weapon of evil. The devil was dead, his heart attack showing the world that in fact, even the devil did, after all, have a heart of sorts. But his tools still abounded on this earth. She found it, apparently flung aside in the desperate haste to catch her. Only then did she dress. She had toyed with the idea of flogging herself. Not in penitence of course, but just to get some small sense of what the Thing was capable of. But now she couldn't do it. It was too perverse even for her. She gingerly picked up the strap. Holy fuck it was heavy. One hit with this and she would have been pleading for him to stop. She shook off the shakes that were starting to come on her again. My god, until this very afternoon, she had never been truly scared of being punished, not like Anne, who was literally terrified of it. Her baby sister must never be allowed to see this or even know that such things existed and were used.

She carried it back into the barn. Where the hell had it been kept? Cristy guessed it didn't really matter, tucked it away in some impossible place that no amount of searching was likely to divulge, and rapidly left the area behind. Besides, why would any investigation search the fucking barn, she thought; it was literally half a mile away from the body. In fact, why should there be any investigation at all? *Old man in summer heat has heart attack*. That's all there is to it, she managed to even smile a little at the simplicity of the thing.

Now yeah, the police might figure out that he was running, by the way he hit the ground. He certainly couldn't have got that bruise in the gut from just keeling over, or could he? The wrist thing was no problem. He was a heavy set man and if he had tried to break his fall, he might well have been injured in that way. But there was nothing she could do about the other now. She had to throw it out to the winds of chance, just as she had done, unbeknownst to herself at the time, about that thing with her mom turning around in mid-flight to see who had pushed her down the stairs.

Cristy was all of a sudden sickish. That *had* been the reason her mom had turned, and she *had* to have known that it was her, her own daughter, that had done the deed. Oh, fuck, I'm gonna throw up, she admitted to herself. Where? Puking out here within sight of the body would be bad. Well, maybe not. She could just claim that she puked when she saw him lying there. So she did, turning her guts out onto the desert of the backyard, watering a minute portion of it with the rest of her conscience as well as her filial piety. Now *that* was a joke, she thought, as she knelt there in the sun, the flies suddenly keeping her company, feasting on her offal. A fucking joke. More mythology shoved down her throat, shoved down all kid's throats, in order to keep the pile of shit they called 'society' clicking over. *That* was what she was staring at, and indeed the flies could have it. She got up, feeling lightheaded, and promptly went inside and lay down. She found she needed water, and maybe some Pepto-Bismol for good measure. These downed, she phoned for help.

The ambulance arrived before Anne and their grandmother had returned, but the attendants not only agreed to leave everything as it was for a little while, they themselves in turn had phoned the sheriff's office to come out for a quick look. The deputy sauntered across the yard to where the ambulance guys were squatting.

"Not much to see here. Poor sod's had a heart attack. Must have been the heat and whatever he was working on out there." The deputy nodded. He turned the body over. "The autopsy should confirm it. Looks like he hurt his hand breaking his fall, maybe a few bruises. He's a heavy load, must have gone down pretty hard."

The deputy was bored. He grunted and told them to take him away. He then turned and stepped toward Cristy, who was sitting on the back porch. She had changed out of her track gear, and was sitting up, head down, hands straight out in front of her, resting on the fine linen of a short summer dress. Sandals with a little heel, hardly designed for running from anything, and a bow in her hair. Just the right look, she thought, to not only charm the professional audience, but to allay Anne's anxieties over what might have happened in her absence. On top of this, it made her feel that she was regaining some of her girlishness and even vulnerability. Now the first she had deliberately discarded ahead of the operation she had just completed, but the second had been plastered all over her face, completely out of her control, for far too much time in its duration. The deputy came up.

"May I sit down, Miss?" Cristy looked up and nodded, giving the handsome fellow a once over that she hoped he wouldn't notice. She put her head down again. "Can you tell me what you saw and when? It's obviously an accident, a heart attack. Your grandfather, I presume?" Cristy nodded without looking up. This was old hat for her now. "So what did you see? Looks like you lost your lunch out there. I understand that." The deputy's voice was very masculine and a little rustic, but he seemed to be gentle enough.

Cristy looked up and into his face. She had prepared her spiel, "I was inside, getting out of the heat. I had been sitting out here, wondering where my grandfather had gotten too. He said he was going out to one of the sheds to fix something, but that was a couple of hours ago. After waiting for quite a while I came out. That was about an hour ago now. I didn't have to go far and I saw him. I didn't get too close. The flies were already humming around his face. There was a lot of blood. I think I almost fainted but I know I fell down and barfed. Then I got up, probably after about thirty minutes, and came inside and phoned them over there." Cristy gestured out towards the ambulance attendants. "I thought maybe somehow he might still be alive and they could save him. I guess I was just dreaming." The deputy sighed.

"I know how it is. You don't have anything to be ashamed about, there was nothing you could do."

"It wasn't as if I knew him hardly at all, its just that, well, we're here, that is, my sister and I, because our parents both died in an accident at the beginning of summer, just maybe eight weeks ago. They didn't pay us much attention neither, but you still feel it. The world is changing and you can't get off it." The deputy was keenly interested. Cristy wondered if she had said far too much.

"You're young and you'll bounce back. I know its hard now, but kids can adapt, way more than adults can. Your sister's younger than you, or older?"

Cristy shook her head and said 'younger'.

"She's going to really need you right now. It'll give you something to focus on other than your own feelings. It'll be good for both of you to take this time to bond with each other in a new way." Was this handsome deputy dude a counselor? He sure was beating the hell out of all the social workers they had met. But he was saying all the right things too, all the things Cristy wanted to hear, all the things she and Anne were already doing. No wonder she began to like him. But she simply nodded.

"I can't tell you any more, sorry about that." Deputy Harrison was immediately up and moving off. He smiled at her gently and said, "Keep your chin up, sweetie. Think of your sister and your future, you'll get through this." Cristy nodded and waved. She suddenly found herself too tired to move, let alone get out of the chair and go back inside. She watched the ambulance guys remove the body, put down some lye against the flies, and drive round the front. They said they would wait until the rest of the family got back. Cristy didn't wait with them. She stayed where she was. The corpse removed, she felt like she was alone again, out back. It was a feeling that began to relax her. She soon fell asleep, there in the warmth of the now mottled sunlight. She even dreamed, and amazingly, her dreams were pleasant.

But they were also short-lived, as she was now being jostled by a soft hand that could only belong to her adorable Anne. She awoke and reached out for her. Anne's face was wet but she was still smiling at her big sister. She asked no questions but took Cristy's head into her arms and pressed it against her chest. She petted it like she was petting a housecat that had taken up near permanent residence in her lap. Presently, Anne said, "they are calling for us." Cristy looked up. She hadn't heard anything at all. Anne repeated herself. "They're calling, we have to go now." What was she talking about? But Cristy found herself unable to voice any thought at all. She got up, as if in a trance, and they rounded the farmhouse together. Out front, the ambulance attendants, the deputy, their grandmother and her friend, the nieces, her grandfather, her mother and father, and some figure dressed in a glowing white robe were all there to greet them. But this greeting was not right. How could these people be here? Who was this figure in white? Cristy looked from one face to the other. All were grim, especially those of her mother and father. She wanted to scream, seeing them standing there, looking at her, but she had again no voice. The white-robed figure closed in on them. Anne had let go of her hand. Cristy had never been so scared. Then:

"Cristy, my hero-princess, my angel-pet, wake up beautiful! You're sleeping beauty, you know that?" This time it was Anne. No, again it was Anne. No, it *was* Anne for real. Cristy found her voice, found she could feel the warmth of the sun and a refreshing breeze had picked up, allaying some of the late afternoon heat. Jesus H. Christ, she *had* been dreaming just then. Cristy thanked god, perhaps ironically, and got up, taking Anne into her arms and giving her the full body treatment. They were almost there now, she thought, regaining her sensibility and shaking off the chill of the dream figures whose memory had left her flesh tingling.

"Where are the others, hot little Anne?" Cristy gave her kid sister a piercingly sweet smile and then kissed her full on the lips, again and then again. Anne responded in kind.

"They're out front. I said I would come round back to find you, and I did!" Anne acted as if it were a true triumph of the will. "I'd leave them there if I could."

Anne was already beginning to play with her, Cristy thought. How magnificent. Yes, let the others head down to the morgue. The two of them could spend the night here, with each other only. God she needed that now, especially now.

As they reached the front, Cristy, shaking off a chill that had overtaken her when she recalled how her recent dream had paid the closest attention to the details of that short journey, found that all was as it should be. No dead people reanimated, no accusatory faces, no robed mysteries ready to pronounce their judgement. Utter nonsense all of it. Cristy sneered at herself this time. 'Shit, I've basically killed three people and I still can't shrug off this garbage'. She was a little disappointed that she still appeared to have a conscience, and a guilty one at that. Her subconscious was merely letting her know the state of the union, such as it was, and she had to grudgingly give it its due. Well, she thought, summoning what little venom that was currently remaining in her emotional glands, maybe it'll be fourth time lucky.

Her grandmother was crying volubly, but had gotten into the ambulance to ride to the hospital. The deputy was satisfied with the ID. Her friend suggested that the nieces, nine and ten respectively, could stay with the older girls while she accompanied Jean to give her moral support. Anne must have showed her displeasure, because the deputy came to the rescue. He would take the younger girls home, after being reassured that the older ones could stay overnight here. Anne said they could. Cristy was impressed. It was the first time that her baby sister had taken command and issued the directives. What a great feeling to have someone else look after things for you, she thought. God, she had never *once* felt that their parents had done so in any way that had helped them Sure, they were good at taking care of things like 'discipline', so-called. But little else it seemed. And in the end, the two little shits couldn't even take care of themselves. They'd been beaten clean by a pair of young teenage girls, their own daughters no less.

Cristy was brooding again. Anne would take care of that as well, starting as soon as these people had gone on their respective ways. Too bad that Gran would be back sooner or later. But Cristy suddenly found herself unable to think ahead and plan. She simply needed a break. The events of today, which no one else would now ever know about, were her burden and hers alone. Carrying them around would feel like a dead weight for a while. She wondered if she could even love her sister as she deserved to be loved right then and there and all through the night. And more than this, love her all through the darkness of night in general, the kind of night that produced dreams of accusation and judgement. But, she stopped herself, what kind of god would sanction the torture of children? What kind of god would allow bigger people to control smaller people just because they could? If there were such a god, Cristy and Anne would find a way to send *him* down the stairs too. Yes, it would have to be a very long flight of stairs, she imagined, but this was what was ultimately necessary. The teacher had told them in her psychology class that some very clever German guy had said that one had to shoot at morals. Cristy didn't understand it at the time, but she was starting to get it now. That dream had helped her, after all. It wasn't specific people that were ultimately the problem, it was the whole fucking shit-headed thing. Now how the fuck do you go about killing that off? Even pushing a god down the stairs wouldn't do

211

it, because after all it was *people*, not gods, who believed in this shit and who acted on it, making it real. And the reality for kids was sometimes hell on earth. The devil, dead or alive, had nothing on people.

But Anne had taken her by the arm and was leading her upstairs. Cristy would let her sister do anything to her just about now, anything to snap her out of this crisis of - what, conscience? Cristy sneered again. Then gave herself up to her sister's tenderness, falling from a dizzy height into her embrace, and taking into her hollowed out interior everything that Anne could give. Falling asleep in her arms, Cristy no longer cared for a world any larger than their shared bed. All of it down the stairs, all of it down. 'S' for stairs. 'S' for satisfaction.

****

The two loving sisters carried on living with their grandmother, she now much more frail and lifeless after the death of her spouse. This was the second time around for her and coming on top of the death of her only daughter, it was almost too much. But the girls kept her going, laboring intensely to keep old Gran from having to do much of anything the next two years or so. And in this time, two things happened which were of note. One, Jean recovered much of her equanimity and her taste for life, and two, she had rewritten her will so that when she passed, the estate and all of its resources and chattel should descend to her granddaughters. It would be held in escrow until Cristy turned eighteen, which was just about a month away now. The girls had grown into young women, but the main immediate effect of this was that their love-making had become lengthier, more complex, and experienced. But as well, their household skills had improved to the point of their Gran suggesting that they begin to manage the farm, maybe even turn it back into a profit making concern. At first this suggestion met with, well, not much. Anne's face turned a blank. Cristy gave her sister a grin and said, "Don't worry, we'll sell it all off and move back to the coast."

All was well, but there was one more little task for Cristy to accomplish. Once again, she didn't take Anne into her confidence. Her baby sister, now almost a sunny and radiant sweet sixteen – just how sweet only her older sister knew – simply woke up one morning to find that her Gramma Jean had passed in the night. The autopsy, such as it was performed given the age of the deceased, revealed that she had simply stopped breathing. A good way to go, said the coroner, the best, in fact. The family lawyer delayed enacting the will long enough for Cristy to inherit without circumlocution. She was now a legal adult. They owned the place, plus all the monies from the sale of their parents' house and vehicles. Plus all the chattel, plus all the shit inside the farmhouse and outbuildings, plus all of the similar smelling material inside of Cristy. But this last would pass in time, she felt. Anne would drain it off, like some festering pus, released from its miasmatic abode down deep in the darkest crevasses of a lost childhood.

They did run the farm as a business for a while. The hired hands keeping their distance when the girls told them they were lesbians. Well, except one, but he ended up having an accident. After that little charade, the sisters sold their stake and moved back to the coast, not to where they had grown up all too quickly but to a rather more isolated area where they live to this day on a large and secluded estate. One night, about a decade after they had moved, Anne rolled over in bed and nestled into her soulmate, whispering, "I never really thanked you for everything you did for us. You saved our lives. You gave me my life back when it had been stolen from me. Don't think I don't know what you did to do this. I will be your adoring slave forever, your servant beyond the grave, my love, I mean it." Cristy had never been more moved. All she could do was hold her baby, her baby sister, now a stunning mid-twenties super-girl. But Anne wasn't finished. "Know this. I would, I will, do the same for you if ever it became necessary. Our love doesn't stop, big sister, our love is our own and nobody shall ever take it from us."

Cristy nodded. She was being transported to another world. She thanked the stars it contained the two of them. The rest of the old world had neither been convinced nor killed off. The most she had been able to do was remove a few minor obstacles and save herself and her sister. She had saved their love, but not love in general. They had their freedom but humanity was still enslaved. In a way, it was as if this whole thing had never happened. But now Anne had wrapped herself around her lithe form and was slowly breathing life back into it. Cristy let herself be taken this way almost every night, hoping each time that the next night she would regain her own ability to love. It hadn't happened yet, but it had only been ten years. She'd get it back, and Anne would be there, waiting for her. She'd get it back. 'L' is for love. 'L' is for 'life'. She'd get them back, she repeated to herself, swooning under Anne's skillful tongue. 'L' is for lips, labia, luscious *Lustigeheit*. But most of all, for love. That was what she had done it all for, Cristy told herself, and it would be worth it in the end, just you wait and see.